# JOSEFINA
## 1824

Second

by Valerie Tripp

✪ American Girl®

03/20

# A Peek into Josefina's World

From the lookout tower, Josefina can spot visitors coming from far away!

Josefina and her family live in New Mexico. Their house is made of *adobe*, a type of hardened earth. Here, the roof and some of the walls are removed to show inside the rooms.

In the middle of the house is an open courtyard with a small garden and two clay ovens.

The house has rooms for sleeping, cooking, eating, weaving, praying, and storage.

# Josefina's Family and Friends

### Papá
Josefina's father, who guides his family with quiet strength

### Ana
Josefina's oldest sister, who is married and has two little boys

### Francisca
Josefina's sixteen-year-old sister, who is headstrong and impatient

### Clara
Josefina's practical, sensible sister, who is thirteen years old

### Antonio and Juan
Ana's little boys, who are three and five

## Tía Dolores
Josefina's aunt, who
has recently come to
stay with her family

## Tía Magdalena
Josefina's godmother,
a respected healer

## Mariana
Josefina's friend,
who lives in the
nearby Indian pueblo

## ʉuelito and Abuelita
Josefina's grandparents,
who live in Santa Fe

## Patrick O'Toole
A scout for an
American wagon train
on the Santa Fe Trail

Josefina and her family speak Spanish, so you'll see some Spanish words in this book. You'll find the meanings and pronunciations of these words in the glossary on page 112. Remember that in Spanish, "j" is pronounced like "h." That means Josefina's name is pronounced "ho-seh-FEE-nah."

# TABLE of CONTENTS

# Spring Sprouts

osefina, your birthday is coming soon, isn't it?" said Tía Dolores.

"*Sí*," said Josefina. She looked up from the loom where she knelt weaving and smiled at her aunt. "I was born on March nineteenth, the feast of San José."

"Well, I think we should have a party," said Tía Dolores. "We'll have several things to celebrate. It's the feast of San José. You will be ten. Spring will be here. And," Tía Dolores added happily, "God willing, we should have quite a lot of new sheep by then. We've made sixty blankets. That's enough to trade for ninety sheep."

"That is good news!" exclaimed Josefina. She and her sisters, Ana, Francisca, and Clara, had worked a long time to make those sixty blankets. First, they had carded the wool and spun it into yarn. Then they dyed the yarn and wove it into long strips of heavy fabric on a loom. Then they sewed the strips together to make blankets.

"It's good," said Clara, carding a tuft of wool to untangle it. "But ninety sheep aren't enough to replace the hundreds that Papá lost in the flood last fall. We can't stop making blankets."

"Oh, baa, baa, baa," Francisca bleated at Clara. "We all know that."

"We wouldn't have any blankets to trade if it weren't for Tía Dolores," said Ana. "It was her idea to turn blankets into sheep."

"I think we should be very proud of ourselves," said Francisca. "Sixty blankets is a lot." She sighed as she poked her needle into the thick cloth. "I know I worked hard on them."

Ana, Clara, and Josefina burst out laughing. Francisca had complained bitterly when Tía Dolores, who came to live with them after Mamá died, announced that the sisters would make blankets to trade for sheep. Now Francisca made it sound as if she were responsible for all sixty blankets!

At first, Francisca scowled at her sisters' laughter. But soon she laughed at herself along with them. "Oh, all right," she admitted grudgingly. "The rest of you worked hard, too."

"Tía Dolores, when do you think Papá will go to the *pueblo* to trade the blankets for Esteban Durán's sheep?" asked Josefina. Esteban, Papá's great friend, was a Pueblo Indian.

"Soon," said Tía Dolores. She smiled at Josefina. "Maybe you'd like to go with him."

Tía Dolores knew that Josefina loved to go to the pueblo and see her friend Mariana, who was Esteban's granddaughter.

"May I find Papá right now and ask him?" Josefina said.

"Sí," said Tía Dolores, who always understood Josefina's eagerness.

"*Gracias!*" said Josefina. She was just about to hurry out the door when an idea stopped her. "Tía Dolores," she said. "Won't you come with me? You should be the one to tell Papá about the blankets and the sheep."

"Very well," laughed Tía Dolores. She put her sewing aside and took Josefina's hand, and together they went out into the cool spring evening.

Josefina loved the way spring came swooping in like a bird on a breeze. At the *rancho,* baby animals were born and plants began to grow. "Look, Tía Dolores," said Josefina. She knelt down and lifted a handful of dead leaves in a corner of the courtyard. Underneath, yellow-green sprouts were sticking up out of the soil. "Pretty soon this whole corner will be full of flowers!"

Tía Dolores knelt, too. Josefina loved the way her aunt never minded getting dirt on her skirt or her hands. "Didn't I tell you?" Tía Dolores said. "Flowers with roots as deep as these your Mamá planted can survive a lot—even a visit from a hungry goat!"

Josefina grinned. She knew that Tía Dolores was talking about Florecita, a mean goat that had bullied and poked her and chewed up Mamá's flowers. "I'll still keep Florecita away from them," she said.

"Don't worry," said Tía Dolores. "Florecita will be too busy to bother your flowers this spring. She's going to have a baby very soon."

"Oh, no!" said Josefina, pretending to groan. "I hope Florecita's baby isn't like her. I don't think I could stand two horrible goats trying to bully me!" Josefina wasn't the least little bit afraid of Floricita anymore, but she didn't like her the least little bit, either.

Josefina and Tía Dolores found Papá in the goat pen. He was sitting next to one of the goats with a lantern at his side.

"Papá," Josefina began excitedly. "Tía Dolores has good news for—" Josefina stopped. She realized that the goat next to Papá was Florecita. But she had never seen Florecita like this. The goat was lying on her side, hardly breathing. Her eyes were shut. "Papá," asked Josefina, "what's wrong?"

"Florecita had her baby tonight," said Papá. "But she's too weak to nurse it. I don't think she'll live."

Living on a rancho, Josefina had seen many animals die. She knew better than to think of the animals as anything more than useful and valuable property. Still, as she looked at her old enemy Florecita, somehow she just couldn't help feeling sorry.

"Can't we do anything?" she asked Papá.

"I don't think so," said Papá.

Florecita's breathing grew slower and slower until at last it stopped. Florecita was dead.

Josefina sighed. "Poor Florecita," she said softly. Then she remembered something important. She turned to Papá. "Where is Florecita's baby?" she asked.

Papá lifted the front corner of his *sarape*. Cradled in his arm was a tiny goat.

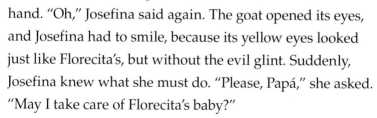

"Oh!" gasped Josefina. Very gently, Josefina reached out and touched the goat's silky little ear. The goat turned its head and nuzzled the palm of Josefina's hand. "Oh," Josefina said again. The goat opened its eyes, and Josefina had to smile, because its yellow eyes looked just like Florecita's, but without the evil glint. Suddenly, Josefina knew what she must do. "Please, Papá," she asked. "May I take care of Florecita's baby?"

Papá's kind face was full of concern. "The baby is very weak, Josefina," he said. "It isn't easy to care for an animal this needy. I think you might be too young for the responsibility. And you must realize that there's a good chance the baby won't live, even if you do care for her," he said to Josefina. "Think how you'll feel if you become fond of the little goat and then she dies."

Josefina understood. Papá was afraid her heart would be broken as it had been when Mamá died. And for a moment, Josefina was afraid, too. But then she looked at the little goat and all her doubts fell away. "I have to try to save Florecita's baby, Papá," she said. "When any of God's creatures is sick or weak, we have to try to make it better, don't we?" She held out her arms for the goat. "Please, Papá," she said.

Papá sighed. Carefully, he put the baby goat into Josefina's arms. She held the soft warm body nestled close to her chest and rubbed her cheek against the goat's fur. The baby goat gave one small bleat, closed her eyes, and went to sleep as if Josefina's arms were the safest place in the world.

"Take her back to the house," said Papá, "and keep her next to the fire. I'll bring some milk. You'll have to teach her to drink. She's yours to care for now."

"I'll take good care of her," said Josefina. "I promise."

That night, Josefina and the baby goat slept on a wide bunk above the kitchen hearth called the shepherd's bed.

Josefina woke up often during the night. She wanted to be sure she could feel the little goat's heart beating and the warmth of its soft breath on her hand.

The little goat made it through the night. Before dawn the next morning, Papá brought Josefina a pouch filled with goat's milk. He attached a rag to the opening of the pouch. The little animal didn't seem to know what to do, so Josefina dipped two fingers in the milk and held them up to its mouth. At first the goat seemed too weak to drink. But then it began to suck the milk off Josefina's fingers. "That's the way," said Josefina. She pressed the milk-soaked rag to the baby goat's mouth. It began to suck on the rag, and soon it eagerly drank all the milk out of the pouch.

"Look, Papá!" said Josefina. "Isn't the baby goat clever?"

"Sí," said Papá. He stroked the goat's head with the back of his finger.

Josefina thought the goat was *very* clever to have figured out how to drink from the pouch!

The baby goat grew stronger as each bright spring day passed. It seemed to thrive on warm sunshine, warm

milk, and Josefina's warm affection. It was not long before the goat was following Josefina everywhere on its quick, sturdy little legs.

"That goat is just like your shadow!" joked Tía Dolores. And so they all began to call the goat Sombrita, which means "little shadow."

Soon everyone was used to seeing Josefina and Sombrita together all over the rancho. As Sombrita grew friskier, Josefina had to keep an eye on her all the time. The rancho was a dangerous place for such a small creature. She might be kicked by a mule or stepped on by an ox. Josefina especially worried about snakes. Snakes were just awakening from their winter hibernation, so they were hungry. In the spring, a rattlesnake was quite likely to strike and kill a baby animal like Sombrita. So Josefina kept Sombrita close by, safe from harm. She had promised to take good care of the little goat, and it was a promise she intended to keep.

# Tía Magdalena

## CHAPTER 2

One warm day, Josefina, her sisters, and Tía Dolores were planting seeds in the garden. Tía Dolores nodded toward Sombrita, who was bleating at the birds flying low near the garden. "Fierce Sombrita is scaring away all the birds trying to steal the seeds."

The sisters laughed, and Sombrita began to show off by kicking up her heels and bleating even louder.

"Who is that noisy animal?" someone asked. It was Tía Magdalena, walking through the gate. She was Papá's older sister, who lived in the village.

The girls and Tía Dolores greeted her politely. Then Tía Dolores answered her question. "That's Sombrita," she said. Her voice was full of fondness and pride as she went on to say, "Josefina has cared for her since she was born. The mother goat died."

"We all thought Sombrita would die, too," said Clara, who was always matter-of-fact. "She was so weak and pitiful."

Tía Magdalena bent down and scooped up Sombrita. She stroked the little goat gently, and Sombrita settled calmly in her arms. Then Tía Magdalena looked at Josefina. "Why did you decide to take care of Sombrita?" she asked.

Josefina didn't know what to say. "I . . . I didn't stop to think about it," she said honestly. "I just . . . I had to, that's all."

"Has it been hard work?" asked Tía Magdalena.

"Oh, no!" said Josefina. "I love taking care of Sombrita!"

"You have done a good job of it," said Tía Magdalena. She handed Sombrita to Josefina. "Sombrita is a fine, healthy goat."

"Gracias, Tía Magdalena," said Josefina. She was pleased to be praised by her aunt. Tía Magdalena was an important person in her family, especially to Josefina, because she was Josefina's godmother. She was an important, respected person in the village, too. Tía Magdalena was the healer, or *curandera*. She knew more about healing than anyone else. People who were injured or ill went to her for care, and she always knew just what to do.

Now Tía Magdalena turned to Tía Dolores. "Here are the mustard leaves you asked for," she said. "Tell your cook Carmen to brew tea from them and give it to her husband, Miguel, to drink if his stomach ache comes back. Please tell her not to use it all at once. I haven't many leaves left. Tansy mustard is usually blooming everywhere by now, but I haven't been able to find any yet this year."

"I've seen some growing by the stream," Josefina
piped up.

"Your young eyes are better than my old ones!" said
Tía Magdalena. "Perhaps you'll gather some leaves for me."
She tilted her head and looked at Josefina as if she were
considering something. "And perhaps when you bring the
leaves, you can stay for a while and help me. My storeroom
needs a spring cleaning."

"Oh, I'd like that very much!" said Josefina.

"Good!" said Tía Magdalena. She smiled, and Josefina
blushed with pride and pleasure. How nice to have pleased
Tía Magdalena!

❋

The very next day Josefina skipped along the road
to the village under a clean blue sky. She had a bunch of
tansy mustard leaves in her hand for Tía Magdalena. Papá,
Tía Dolores, and the sisters were going to the village, too.
Josefina had left Sombrita behind under Carmen's watchful
eye. Josefina missed Sombrita, but she knew the little goat
would only be in the way today. In the morning, the men
and boys were going to clean out the water ditches, called
*acequias,* while the women and girls replastered the church.
And in the afternoon, Josefina would be too busy to keep
an eye on Sombrita when she went to help Tía Magdalena.

Most of the villagers had already gathered in the *plaza*

at the center of the village when Josefina and her family arrived. They called out greetings. *"Buenos días!"*

"Buenos días," Papá replied. "It's a fine day to work, by God's grace."

"It is," said Señor Sánchez, who was in charge of the water ditches. "Let's begin." He and Papá and the other men and boys shouldered their tools and set off to work. Clearing the acequias was a very important springtime job. Later in the spring, when the snow on the mountaintops melted, the acequias had to be clear of leaves and sticks and weeds so that the water could flow to the fields. Without water, nothing planted that spring would grow.

*acequia*

"We'd better begin our work, too," said Señora Sánchez. The women and girls agreed. They took off their shoes, rolled up their sleeves, covered their hair, and tucked up their skirts. Replastering the church was another important chore. It was normally done later in the spring. But because the weather had been so unusually warm the past few weeks, the women were replastering much earlier this year.

Josefina was glad. As she scooped up a handful of gritty mud plaster, she decided replastering was a chore that was fun.

"Watch out!" Josefina shouted to Clara, who stood

between her and the church. Clara ducked, and Josefina flung her handful of mud plaster at the wall of the church, where it stuck—*splat*—in a glob.

Clara laughed, saying, "You'll splatter mud all over if you do it that way." Clara was neat. She pressed her handful of mud plaster against the wall.

But even Clara was easygoing today, thought Josefina as she spread the glob of mud over the *adobe* bricks so that it was smooth and even. The women and girls gossiped and chattered as they worked. The very oldest ladies sat in the shade, keeping an eye on the babies. They called out jokes and encouragement to the others. Every once in a while someone would start a song and everyone would join in. Voices high and low, in tune and out of tune, rose up from all around the church.

Josefina liked making the church walls whole again. Later, she and some other children climbed up onto the roof to spread a new layer of mud plaster on it as well. Josefina loved the feeling of the mud oozing between her bare toes. It was exhilarating to be up high, closer to the huge white clouds and the brilliant blue sky. Josefina and the others shrieked with joy as they slipped and slid on the slick mud to tamp it flat.

"Josefina!" Clara called out. She was standing below on the ground, looking up, shading her eyes with her hand.

*Clara ducked, and Josefina flung her handful of mud plaster at the wall of the church, where it stuck—**splat**—in a glob.*

"Tuck your skirt up higher in the back or you'll get mud on it and look messy at Tía Magdalena's this afternoon."

"And pull up your *rebozo* so that it shades your face," Francisca added. "Your nose is getting as red as a tomato."

Josefina looked down at tidy, sensible Clara and at beautiful Francisca, who was fussy about her skin. She knew that right now her sisters envied her. *They* were too old to be on the roof.

*Almost ten is a wonderful age to be,* thought Josefina, exuberantly slooshing her feet through the mud. *I'm not too old to slip and slide on the roof, and yet I am old enough to take care of Sombrita and old enough to help Tía Magdalena!* She waved to her sisters and cheerfully ignored their advice.

❈

"Bless you, child!" said Tía Magdalena that afternoon, when she saw Josefina at her door with a bouquet of mustard leaves. "Come in!"

"Gracias," said Josefina. She stepped inside and took a deep breath. Nowhere else on earth smelled quite the way Tía Magdalena's house smelled. Mixed in with the scent of flowers was the sharp, nose-tickling scent of spices and the musty, earthy tang of the herbs that hung upside down in bunches from the beams.

Tía Magdalena smiled when she saw

Josefina looking up at the herbs. "You'd like to know how to use them, wouldn't you?" she asked.

Josefina nodded, wondering how Tía Magdalena knew.

"The mint leaves ease stomach aches. The pennyroyal brings a fever down. I use the *manzanilla* flowers to make a tea to cure a baby's colic," Tía Magdalena said, pointing to each herb as she named it. "And speaking of babies, how is your sweet Sombrita today?"

"She's *very* well, thank you," answered Josefina, smiling.

"She's *very* fortunate to have you caring for her!" said Tía Magdalena. She looked merry. Tía Magdalena was much older than Papá. Her gray hair was streaked with white. But when she smiled as she did now, her expression was lively. "Now, we must do some work," she said. "Come with me."

Tía Magdalena led Josefina to the small storeroom at the back of her house. Along one wall were shelves lined with jars of all shapes and sizes. Tía Magdalena tilted her head toward the jars. "Here's where I need your help," she said to Josefina. Her eyes sparkled. "Why don't we make a game of it? You lift a jar down from the shelf, look inside, and see if you can guess what's in it. I'll dust the jar, you dust the shelf, and then you can put the jar back. All right?"

"Sí!" said Josefina. She reached for the biggest, most

important-looking jar of all. It was blue-and-white china.

"Oh, not that jar!" said Tía Magdalena. "It's empty."

"It looks very old," said Josefina.

"Indeed it is. It's probably the oldest thing in this house. It's even older than I am!" Tía Magdalena joked. "It's an apothecary jar. I don't know how it came to be in our village, but I know that it's been here for more than a hundred years. The woman who was curandera before I was gave it to me. She got it from the woman who was curandera before her. Long ago, I believe, there was a whole set of jars like it. That's the only one left." Tía Magdalena pointed to a smaller jar next to the blue-and-white one. "Let's start with that jar instead," she said.

Josefina took the smaller jar off the shelf and looked inside. "It looks like pumpkin stems," she said. "Could it be?"

"Sí," said Tía Magdalena. "You're sharp to recognize them." She dusted the jar as Josefina dusted the shelf. "There's nothing in the world better for a sore throat," she said. "You toast the pumpkin stem, grind it to a powder, mix it with fat and salt, and rub it on the throat inside and out."

Josefina enjoyed helping Tía Magdalena. Every jar

held something that Tía Magdalena used as a remedy. There was dried deer blood to be mixed with water and drunk for strength. There was vinegar so strong that it made Josefina's eyes water. It was used as a soak to stop infections. Another jar held a terrible-smelling herb that was used to soothe achy joints. Josefina guessed what was in many of the jars. But some she didn't recognize.

"What is this?" she asked Tía Magdalena.

"That's the root of a globe mallow plant," said Tía Magdalena. "I crush it and make a paste to put on a rattlesnake bite to draw out the poisonous venom." She handed one of the roots to Josefina. "Put that in your pouch and take it home with you," she said with a mischievous look. "And someday, ask your papá if he recognizes it."

"Papá?" asked Josefina.

"Sí," said Tía Magdalena. "Once, when he was a boy just about your age, he was guarding the sheep. He tried to scare away a rattlesnake by hitting it with a pebble from his sling. He missed. The snake got mad and bit him. Your papá killed the snake with a rock before he came to me for help. That was very brave, but very foolish of him! If you don't get the venom out right away, it can kill you." She shook her head. "I'll never forget the sight of him coming toward me, so proud of his own courage, and with that dead snake slung over his shoulders!"

Josefina put the root in her pouch and shuddered. She hated even *hearing* about snakes! But she liked to hear Tía Magdalena tell stories about Papá when he was a boy.

"Your papá was always too fearless and too stubborn for his own good," Tía Magdalena said as she dusted a jar. "And too quiet. But that didn't matter when your mamá was alive. She knew what he was thinking anyway."

Josefina was surprised at how easy it was to talk to Tía Magdalena about Mamá as they worked. "Sometimes it seems so long ago that Mamá died," Josefina said.

"Sometimes it seems like it just happened. And sometimes I'll see Mamá in a dream, and it seems as if she's still with us."

"Sí," said Tía Magdalena. Her old brown eyes seemed to see right into Josefina's heart. "That is how it is always going to be for you."

"Sí," said Josefina, running her cloth over a shelf to dust it. "And for Papá, too, I think. He's not quite so quiet and sad as he was just after Mamá died. It has been better for us all since Tía Dolores came. We needed her."

"Well," said Tía Magdalena, handing a jar to Josefina. "Perhaps *she* needed *you,* too."

Josefina wondered what Tía Magdalena meant. But just then, Tía Magdalena said, "I think it's time for a cup of tea, don't you?" And so Josefina didn't have a chance to ask.

# Second Chances

hen they were seated with their tea and some sweet cookies, Tía Magdalena said, "You've done well today."

"Gracias," said Josefina. "I was glad to help." She sipped her hot mint tea and gathered her courage to say what she was thinking. "I've really enjoyed helping you this afternoon," she said. "And I was thinking . . . I was thinking that I'd like to be a curandera. Do you think you could teach me when I'm old enough?"

When Tía Magdalena answered, her voice was kind. "You can't simply choose to be a curandera," she said. "You have to know which herbs cure which ills, and you have to be observant and careful. But more than all that, you must be a healer."

"A healer," repeated Josefina. "How will I know if I'm a healer or not?"

"You'll know," said Tía Magdalena. "You'll know. It will be clear to you and to everyone else if you are."

While Tía Magdalena cleared up after their tea, Josefina went back to the storeroom to finish dusting. All the while, she was remembering what Tía Magdalena had said. How she wished there were some way to prove to Tía Magdalena that she was the right kind of person to be a curandera!

Josefina looked at the big blue-and-white jar on the shelf and thought about how it had been handed down from curandera to curandera. The jar was dusty. Surely Tía Magdalena would be pleased if she dusted it as a surprise for her. Josefina stood on her tiptoes to take the jar off the shelf. She could reach it with only one hand. She tapped the jar to move it to the edge of the shelf so that she could lift it off with both hands and . . . CRASH!

The jar fell to the floor and smashed into a thousand pieces. Josefina's heart stopped beating. For a terrible moment she stood still, staring in horror at what she had done. Then, without thinking, Josefina ran from the room. She flew past Tía Magdalena, out the door, and ran away as fast as she could.

*Shame, shame, shame!* The word pounded in Josefina's head with every step she took. Josefina ran all the way to the orchard. She climbed up into her favorite apricot tree. *How could I have been so clumsy?* she thought. *Tía Magdalena treasured the blue-and-white jar, and I destroyed it. Then I ran away! What a stupid, childish thing to do! I'll never be able to face Tía Magdalena again!*

Josefina clung to the tree trunk, and hot tears ran down her cheeks. She had been sitting that way for a while when she heard someone say, "Josefina?"

Josefina looked down through the branches and saw Tía Dolores's face lifted toward her. Josefina felt as if all her bones had melted. She slid down from the tree right into Tía Dolores's arms and buried her face in Tía Dolores's shoulder. Then she cried and cried. Tía Dolores rubbed her back and let her cry. When at last her sobs stopped, Tía Dolores put a cool hand on Josefina's cheek and looked at her with sympathetic eyes.

"Your papá went to Tía Magdalena's house to walk home with you," said Tía Dolores. "She told him what happened, and he told me."

"Is Tía Magdalena angry?" asked Josefina. "And Papá, too?"

Tía Dolores smoothed Josefina's hair and said, "They're sad and . . ."

"And disappointed," Josefina finished for her. Roughly, Josefina wiped the tears off her cheeks and said, "I broke Tía Magdalena's most precious jar. Then I made it worse by running away. I ruined everything."

"Everything?" asked Tía Dolores.

Josefina was so ashamed and miserable that she could hardly speak. "I was hoping Tía Magdalena would teach me to be a curandera when I am old enough," Josefina said. "Now she won't want to."

"Ah, I see," said Tía Dolores. "Can you tell me why you want to be a curandera?"

"I like helping people feel better," Josefina said. "And I've ... I've always wondered if there's a reason why Mamá chose Tía Magdalena to be my godmother. Maybe Mamá hoped I'd be a curandera."

"You mean, maybe she had the same hope for you that you have for yourself," said Tía Dolores. She hugged Josefina and said, "You know what you must do right now, don't you?"

"Sí," said Josefina. "Sweep up the mess I made, and apologize to Tía Magdalena."

"And you must ask her to give you a second chance," said Tía Dolores.

Josefina sighed hopelessly.

"Spring is the season for second chances," said Tía Dolores. "Didn't your mamá's flowers sprout again? Didn't Sombrita get another chance to live when you promised to take care of her?" Tía Dolores smiled. "We're all given second chances. We just have to be brave enough to take them."

Josefina hugged Tía Dolores. She hoped Tía Dolores was right. Oh, if Tía Magdalena would give her a second chance, she would be so grateful!

✸

Tía Magdalena had only one thing to say after Josefina apologized. "The jar cannot be repaired," she said. "But perhaps your hopes can."

✸

Whenever Josefina made up her mind to do something, it cheered her. She felt awful about what she had done at Tía Magdalena's. But she wasn't going to let her mistake kill her hopes. She still wanted to be a healer. Tía Magdalena had said that it would be clear to her and to everyone else if she were. She was determined to find out. Josefina kept the root Tía Magdalena had given her in her pouch as a reminder to herself.

The weather was cold and rainy, as if winter had returned. But finally, just the day before Josefina's birthday, the clouds brightened from gray to white and the sun shone. On that spring morning full of promise, Josefina set out with Papá and his servant Miguel to go to the pueblo.

Papá and Miguel were leading mules that were loaded down with blankets. Josefina couldn't help feeling proud

when she looked at the blankets. She had made some of them, and now Papá was going to trade them to his friend Esteban.

Josefina had another reason to be happy. She was going to see *her* friend

Mariana, Esteban's granddaughter. Josefina had tucked her doll, Niña, into her sash because Mariana liked to play dolls. And of course she'd brought along her faithful little shadow, Sombrita, to meet Mariana.

The pueblo was five long miles downstream from the rancho, and after the first mile Sombrita lagged. Josefina had to pick her up and carry her. Josefina was relieved when the stream widened and the pueblo seemed to appear all of a sudden. It rose up between the stream and the mountains. The pueblo was made of adobe just as Josefina's house was. But it was much taller than Josefina's house because several stories were built one on top of the other. Ladders led from level to level.

*pueblo*

When Papá, Josefina, and Miguel arrived at the pueblo, they entered its big, clean-swept center plaza. Esteban met them at his doorway. "Welcome," he said to Papá.

"Gracias," answered Papá. "May God bless you."

Miguel began to unload the blankets from the mules. Sombrita stayed with Miguel as Esteban led Papá and Josefina inside. They sat down by the fire, and almost immediately Mariana and her grandmother appeared with bowls of food and cups of hot tea. Mariana didn't say anything, but she smiled shyly at Josefina and her eyes had a welcome in them. Josefina smiled back. Both girls knew they shouldn't speak unless one of the grown-ups asked them a question. It wouldn't be good manners.

As they ate, Papá and Esteban talked about the weather, their crops, and their animals. Even though both men knew Papá had come to trade, they didn't talk about it. To begin by talking about business would be rude.

But Josefina was impatient. She couldn't wait to show Sombrita to Mariana. Josefina tried to sit as still as her friend did, but it was hard. At last Papá and Esteban finished their food.

"My friend," said Esteban, "thank you for bringing the blankets."

"Thank you for accepting them," said Papá. "I've brought sixty."

"Good," said Esteban. "When the sheep are old enough, I'll drive them to your rancho."

Papá nodded. This was the way he and Esteban had always traded. Nothing was written. Esteban's spoken promise was enough. Papá said that his family and Esteban's family had always respected each other and traded with each other fairly.

Josefina knew that this summer both Papá and Esteban were going to trade for the first time with the *americanos* who came to Santa Fe from the United States. Papá planned to trade mules, and Esteban would trade the blankets that Josefina and Papá had brought to him today.

"I hope trading with the americanos will be a good thing," Papá said.

Esteban nodded to show that he shared Papá's hope.

Then Mariana caught her grandfather's eye, and he smiled. Both Josefina and Mariana knew that was a sign that they could go. They stood up eagerly and hurried outside into the sunshine. Josefina picked up Sombrita and held her to face Mariana. "This is my Sombrita," she said. "We call her that because she follows me like a shadow wherever I go."

"Oh!" sighed Mariana. Her eyes were wide with delight. "Will Sombrita follow us to the stream?" Mariana asked.

"Of course!" said Josefina. "Watch!"

As Josefina and Mariana walked toward the stream, they peeked over their shoulders from time to time and shared a giggle at the sight of Sombrita following right on their heels. When they reached the stream, the girls found a sunny spot to play. Sombrita curled up in the warm grass and went to sleep. Josefina took her doll, Niña, out of her sash. Mariana had a doll, too, made out of cornhusks. The girls pretended that their dolls were sisters. They made necklaces for them out of tiny wildflowers and boats from curves of bark.

They had just launched
their boats in the stream
when suddenly Josefina
stood up. "Where is
Sombrita?" she asked
Mariana. "I don't see her."
Mariana stood up, too.
The girls shaded their eyes and
looked all around. But the little
black-and-white goat was nowhere to be seen. "We'll have
to look for her," said Josefina. "She can't have gone very
far." She tucked Niña into her sash and Mariana picked up
her doll, and they walked along the narrow footpath that
led downstream. Josefina hoped they were going in the
right direction. She could still see the pueblo behind them,
but it seemed to shrink smaller with every step they took.
Both girls knew they should not be so far from the pueblo,
but they *had* to find little Sombrita. They couldn't stop. The
farther they went, the faster they walked, and the more
worried they both became.

With anxious steps, the girls kept going. Just after
they'd rounded another bend in the path, Josefina
squinted. She thought she saw something black and white
in the grass ahead. Could it be? It was! Josefina's heart
lifted. "Oh, Sombrita," she cried as she ran forward.

Sombrita didn't look at her. The goat was staring at something else with friendly curiosity, as if it might be a delightful new plaything.

When Josefina saw what it was, she stopped short. All her relief turned to horror. Between her and the little goat was a huge rattlesnake.

Josefina swallowed hard. She felt sweat on her forehead and an odd trembling in her stomach. The snake was coiled and ready to strike. Josefina heard its eerie rattle. She saw its scary, skinny tongue darting in and out of its mouth. She saw the snake's beady black eyes in their sunken sockets. Josefina bit her lip. The snake's cruel stare was fixed on Sombrita.

# Rattlesnake!

osefina," said Mariana in a low voice. She saw the snake, too.

Josefina signaled Mariana to stay back. She had only one thought. *She had to save Sombrita!* Ever so slowly, Josefina sank down and picked up a rock. She held it out behind her to Mariana. Mariana understood and silently stretched out her hand to take it.

When their hands touched, Josefina whispered, "I'm going to get Sombrita. Don't throw the rock unless the snake moves, because if you miss..."

Mariana squeezed Josefina's hand and then took the rock.

Very, very slowly, Josefina edged forward. She made a wide arc around the snake. Inch by anxious inch she moved closer to Sombrita, who, for once, stood still. Josefina stooped, gathered Sombrita in her arms, and straightened. Then everything happened so fast it was a blur. The snake gave a menacing rattle. Mariana threw the rock at it and missed. The snake whipped its head around, shot forward, and struck Mariana on the arm with its fangs.

*Josefina stooped and gathered Sombrita in her arms.*

"Mariana!" cried Josefina as she saw her friend grab her arm and stumble back. Suddenly furious, Josefina put Sombrita down and snatched up a rock. She threw with all her might. The rock hit the snake in its middle. With one last sickening hiss, the snake slithered away so fast, it seemed to simply disappear.

Mariana moaned, sinking to her knees as if all the strength had gone out of her. She didn't cry, but her breath was ragged. Her eyes were shut tight.

Josefina bent over her friend. "Let me see your arm," she said. Gently, Josefina took Mariana's arm in her hands. She couldn't help gasping when she saw two tiny holes where the snake's fangs had sunk in. The wound was an ugly purplish color, and it was already beginning to swell. In her mind, Josefina heard Tía Magdalena's voice saying, *If you don't get the venom out right away, it can kill you.* Josefina spoke with urgency to Mariana. "We've got to get back to the pueblo," she said. "We need help."

Mariana tried to stand but dropped back to her knees. "I can't . . . I can't go that far," she said in a hoarse whisper.

Josefina's heart twisted with fear. She knelt down and something hard in her pouch thunked against her hip. It was the globe mallow root Tía Magdalena had given her. Without hesitating, Josefina took it out. She crushed the root between two rocks and spit on it to make it pasty.

Then she pressed it against Mariana's arm
where the snake had struck. She squeezed
Mariana's arm gently to bring the venom up.
Mariana whimpered, but she didn't pull her arm away.

Again and again, Josefina pressed the crushed root
against the wound. Again and again, she pressed Mariana's
arm. Again and again and again . . . Josefina knew she had
to stay calm, but she had to fight against a rising feeling
of panic. The globe mallow didn't seem to be working!
Mariana's arm was still swollen and bruised-looking. Oh,
how long would it take? What if she was using the root the
wrong way? Perhaps she had misunderstood. What would
happen to Mariana if the venom poisoned her blood? If
only someone would come to help!

But no one came. The minutes felt like hours. Josefina
was just about to give up and run for help when—oh, at
last!—she heard Mariana take a deep, shuddery breath.
Mariana opened her eyes, and color came back to her face.

Josefina said a quick, silent prayer of thanks. Then she
asked Mariana, "Do you think you can walk if I help you?"

Mariana nodded.

Carefully, Josefina helped Mariana stand. Mariana
looped her good arm over Josefina's shoulder, and Josefina
put her own arm behind Mariana's back to support her.
"Lean on me," Josefina said. Then she turned and looked

down at Sombrita. "Listen," she said to the little goat. "Now you must really be my *sombrita,* my little shadow. Stay right behind me. Do you understand?"

Sombrita seemed to understand. She stayed close to Josefina and Mariana every step of the weary walk back. Slowly, the two girls trudged along the path next to the stream and up the long incline to the pueblo.

Papá and Esteban rushed to the girls, and Josefina saw that their faces were tight with worry. Mariana said quickly, "A rattlesnake bit me, but Josefina knew what to do." She smiled weakly at Josefina. "Tell them," she said.

Papá and Esteban stared at Josefina, but she was too worn out to explain. Instead she held out her hand to show them the crushed root. "It draws the venom out," she said. "I had it in my pouch."

Esteban's expression did not change. His voice was very deep when he said, "Gracias, Josefina. Gracias." He lifted Mariana up. Papá, Josefina, and Sombrita followed them the rest of the way back to the pueblo.

Later, as they were walking home to the rancho, Papá asked Josefina to tell him the whole story of what had happened. So Josefina did. She didn't leave out anything, even though she was out of breath because she had to take two steps for every one of Papá's. They hadn't gone very far before Papá lifted both Josefina and Sombrita up onto a mule's back. After that Josefina couldn't see Papá's face, but somehow she knew that he was still listening hard to every word she said.

❀

Josefina opened one sleepy eye. Could she be dreaming? It was not quite dawn, and yet she seemed to hear music. She sat up. Her sisters Francisca and Clara were gone from the room that they shared with her. Suddenly, Josefina grinned to herself. She remembered what day it was: the feast day of San José and her birthday.

Very slowly, the door to her room opened. In the pearly morning light she saw Papá, Tía Dolores, Ana and her husband Tomás, Francisca, Clara, Carmen, and her husband Miguel. They all began to sing:

*On the day you were born*
*All the beautiful flowers were born,*
*The sun and moon were born,*
*And all the stars.*

In the middle of the song, Sombrita poked her head around the corner of the door and bleated as if she were singing, too. Everyone laughed, and Tía Dolores said, "We wanted to surprise you with a lovely morning song, but

I think someone forgot the words!"

Josefina picked up Sombrita and gave her a hug. "Gracias," she said to everyone, feeling a little shy at all the attention. "I liked it."

That night, the party table looked elegant. There was a beautiful cloth on it, and the family's best plates and glasses and silverware. Tía Dolores had made a special fancy loaf of bread. There were meat turnovers, and fruit tarts, and candied fruit that looked like jewels. But best of all, in the center of the table there was a red jar with one small branch of apricot blossoms in it. Josefina smiled as she remembered the day Tía Dolores had comforted her next to that apricot tree. *We're all given second chances*, Tía Dolores had said. *We just have to be brave enough to take them.*

Soon music and laughter and happy voices swirled around the beautiful table. Friends and neighbors and workers from the rancho arrived with small gifts of dried fruit or nuts, sweets, or chocolate for Josefina. Esteban and Mariana brought a wonderful gift. It was a melon that had been buried in sand since last fall's harvest to keep it fresh.

When Josefina thanked her, Mariana said, "It's not much, but my heart goes with it."

Papá quieted everyone. "Today is the feast of San José," he said, "and today my daughter Josefina is ten years old. I'm going to tell you a story about her." Josefina felt

Mariana's hand slip into her own. They both stood still, eyes shyly cast down, while Papá told the story of the rattlesnake. Papá began at the beginning and told everything that had happened. He described the snake in such a scary way that it made everyone shiver. When he finished the story, Papá called Josefina to him. He leaned down to kiss Josefina's cheek. "I am proud of you," he said. Josefina thought she had never in her life felt so happy.

Suddenly, Tía Magdalena was by her side. "Dear child," she said. "I think you found out that you are a healer."

"Sí," Josefina said simply. "I am."

❋

Later that evening, when the party was over, Josefina and Papá walked to the goat pen together. They wanted to check on Sombrita, who had not been invited to the party. Sombrita was fast asleep.

"It's unusual to see her so still, isn't it?" said Papá. "Usually she's full of life. She might not have been, if you hadn't kept your promise to take care of her after Florecita died. You gave her a second chance at life."

"Papá," said Josefina. "We're all given second chances. We just have to be brave enough to take them. That's what Tía Dolores says."

"Does she?" asked Papá. "Does she indeed?"

# The Bird-Shaped Flute

## CHAPTER 5

H igh up on a breezy hilltop, Josefina sat playing her clay flute. The flute was shaped like a bird and sounded like one, too. When Josefina played it, a clear, fine tune just like a bird's whistle looped through the air into the blue, blue sky.

The soft days of spring had flown by swiftly, and now it was July. Josefina and her family were visiting her grandfather's rancho, which was about a mile from the center of Santa Fe. Josefina loved this hilltop behind Abuelito's house. From here she could see the flat rooftops of buildings in Santa Fe and the narrow streets that zigzagged between them. She could see the slender silvery ribbon that was the Santa Fe River, and the long road that led home to Papá's rancho fifteen miles away.

A few days ago Josefina, Papá, Francisca, Clara, and Tía Dolores had traveled on that road to come to Abuelito's rancho. The trip was hot and dusty, but Josefina had been too excited to mind. She and her family had worked, planned, and looked forward to the trip for almost a year.

They were traveling for a very important reason. They

needed to be in Santa Fe when the wagon train from the
United States arrived. Papá had brought mules and more
blankets with him to trade with the americanos. Josefina
understood how much depended on this trade. If the
americanos paid well for the mules and the blankets, Papá
would be able to replace his sheep that had been killed
in the terrible flood last fall. If Papá could not replace the
sheep, it would be a hard, hungry winter for everyone on
the rancho. They needed sheep for food and for wool to
weave. Josefina had prayed and prayed that Papá's trading
with the americanos would go well.

Josefina and her sisters couldn't wait to see the new, fine
and fancy things the americanos would bring. Just now,
though, Josefina *heard* something new. It sounded as if a real
bird were singing along with her clay flute. Josefina stopped
playing and tilted her head to listen. Then she grinned. It
wasn't a real bird at all. It was a person whistling.

"Buenos días!" Josefina called out. She turned, expect-
ing to see that the whistler was one of her sisters. But the
whistler was a young man Josefina had never seen before.
Josefina scrambled to her feet so quickly that she almost
dropped her flute. She immediately folded her hands,
bowed her head, and looked down at the ground, which
was the polite way for a child to stand before an adult. She
could tell just by looking at the tips of the stranger's boots

that they came from the United States. She knew because Abuelito had a pair of boots like them that he'd bought last summer from the americanos.

"Buenos días," said the young man. He spoke in Spanish, but with an accent Josefina had never heard before.

Josefina had a sudden, excited thought. The young man must be an americano who'd come ahead of the wagon train! She raised her eyes and sneaked a peek. He had a very *nice* face, Josefina decided. He had blue eyes, a sun-burned nose, and a friendly smile.

"Forgive me for surprising you," the stranger went on. "I thought you were a bird."

*I thought you were a bird, too!* Josefina almost said. She wanted to ask, *Please, señor, who* are *you?* But of course she didn't. It wasn't good manners for a child to ask questions of a grown-up. In fact, Josefina wasn't sure whether it was proper for her to talk to the stranger at all. Perhaps she should act like a bird and fly away! But that didn't seem very polite.

While Josefina stood wondering what she should do, the young man did something astonishing. He took a case off his back, opened it, took out a violin, and began to play. Josefina smiled when she realized that he was playing the same notes that she had played on her flute. The young man wound the notes together into a tune that danced in

*"Forgive me for surprising you," the stranger said.
"I thought you were a bird."*

the air. When he finished, he swept his hat off his head
and bowed. "I'm Patrick O'Toole, from Missouri," he said.
"What is your name?"

"By God's grace," Josefina answered, "I am Josefina
Montoya."

"Josefina Montoya," Patrick repeated slowly. "I'm glad
to meet you. I'm looking for the home of Señor Felipe
Romero. Do you know him?"

"Sí," answered Josefina politely. "He's my grandfather."
She pointed to Abuelito's house nearby. "He lives right
there."

"Well, then, Señorita Josefina," said Patrick as he put
his violin away. "Will you lead me to your grandfather's
house?"

"I will," answered Josefina. "Please, follow me."

Abuelito's house was built around a center courtyard.
The doors to the kitchen, the sleeping rooms, the weaving
room, and the family *sala* opened to it. Josefina led
Patrick across the courtyard to the
family sala, where her family
was gathering for the midday
meal. Abuelito had come to
the door and was staring out at her.

"Abuelito," Josefina said respectfully, "please permit me
to introduce Señor Patrick O'Toole, from—" Josefina

pronounced the English word carefully—"Missouri."

"*Bienvenido,*" Abuelito said to Patrick. "You are welcome in my house, young man. Please come in."

"Thank you, sir," said Patrick.

"Please sit and have something to eat, señor," said Abuelita generously. "Honor us by joining us."

"Gracias," said Patrick.

Josefina sat between Francisca and Clara. Both sisters poked her and looked at her with raised eyebrows that said silently in sister language, *Oh, we can't wait to find out how you met the americano!* Josefina grinned back, pleased to have made her sisters curious.

During the meal, Abuelito kept the conversation away from business. He spoke to Patrick about the beautiful summer weather they were having and asked Patrick about weather in Missouri. Abuelita said nothing, but her sharp eyes never left Patrick's face. Papá didn't say anything either. But Josefina could tell that he was listening carefully to everything Patrick said.

*I hope Papá likes Señor Patrick,* Josefina thought. *I hope everyone does.* She was glad when Tía Dolores said to

Patrick, "You speak Spanish well. How did you learn?"

"My father taught me," said Patrick. "I can't read or write Spanish at all, and I'm afraid I don't always remember the right words to say."

"You are doing fine," said Abuelito kindly.

Finally everyone had finished eating and the servants had cleared the table. Abuelito turned to Patrick. "Now," he said. "Tell us. When will the wagon train arrive?"

"Tomorrow morning, sir," said Patrick.

"That's good news!" said Abuelito. "But how is it that you are here before the rest of the wagon train?"

"I'm one of the scouts," explained Patrick. "Scouts ride ahead of the wagon train. We find the safest places to cross rivers, the easiest passes through the mountains, and the best places to set up camp along the way. I'll be here in Santa Fe for about a week. I have to be ready to leave at a moment's notice. As soon as the captain of the wagon train gives me the word, I'll be heading down the Camino Real. Many of the americano traders are continuing farther south into Mexico when they leave Santa Fe, so the scouts have to go ahead of them and explore the route. Anything you can tell me would be a great help, Señor Romero."

"It will be a pleasure," said Abuelito.

"Thank you, sir," said Patrick. "Maybe you can help me in another way, too. The traders will need fresh mules for their trip down the Camino Real. They asked me to find some. Do you know anyone who has mules to sell or trade?"

Papá spoke slowly. "I have mules to trade," he said.

"Oh!" said Patrick. "May I see them, Señor Montoya?"

Papá nodded. "You may see them," he said. "Come with me." Papá stood and gestured toward the door. Patrick politely thanked Abuelita for her hospitality.

After they left, Clara said, "You and the americano seem to have become acquainted very quickly, Josefina."

"Too quickly," said Abuelita, frowning. "We don't really know this americano at all. How do we know he is honest? All we know for certain is that he's very young. I hope your papá will be careful. I don't think it's wise to trust a stranger, especially when the business is so important!"

"Nothing is decided yet," said Tía Dolores quietly.

Abuelita went on. "If this young man isn't reliable, it'll be a terrible mistake to do business with him," she said.

Abuelita sighed and Josefina's shoulders drooped. She had been so proud to be the one who brought Patrick to her family! Would Papá be wrong to trust Patrick? Was she wrong to like Patrick?

# Heart's Desire

## CHAPTER 6

**T**his is a day I'll remember as long as I live, thought Josefina. She was holding Tía Dolores's hand, waiting for the wagon train to pull into town. *Any minute now,* thought Josefina with a delighted shiver. *Any minute!*

Suddenly, someone shouted, "The wagons! The americanos! The wagon train is here!" Around Josefina, many people were clapping, cheering, and waving as the americanos' wagons lumbered into view. But other people were not so enthusiastic. They stood quietly, arms crossed over their chests, as if they were not convinced that the arrival of the americanos was a good thing.

Josefina stood on tiptoe to see the wagons better. But she didn't let go of Tía Dolores's hand. "Look how big the wagons are!" she said. The wagons *were* enormous. Their wheels stood higher than Josefina's head!

Papá bent toward Tía Dolores so she could hear him above the hubbub. "Abuelito and I are going to look for Señor Patrick at the customs house," he said. "The

americanos have to go there to make a list of their goods and
to pay taxes. The servant will stay with you and the girls."

Tía Dolores nodded. "Very well," she said. "Go ahead."

Then Tía Dolores turned to Josefina and her sisters.
Her eyes were shining. "Your papá and I think that you
girls deserve something for all the hard work you've done
weaving," she said. "We've decided that you may each
choose one of the blankets you wove, and you may sell it
or trade it for anything you wish."

"*Oh!*" gasped Francisca and Clara. "How wonderful!"

Josefina didn't say anything. Instead, she hugged Tía
Dolores. Josefina and her sisters had never expected to use
the blankets they'd woven to get anything for themselves.
*It's just like Tía Dolores to think of something so generous*,
thought Josefina.

"Well!" said Francisca. She had an eager gleam in her
eyes. "Let's decide what we'll get with our blankets!"

Never in her life had Josefina imagined such a variety
of things. She saw bolts of brightly colored cottons, wools,
and silks. There were shoes and hats, boots and stockings,
combs, brushes, toothbrushes, and even silver toothpicks!

Clara stood for a long time studying pots and pans until
Francisca dragged her away to look at buttons and jewelry
she saw sparkling ahead. Clara stopped halfway there to
gaze at knitting needles. Tía Dolores was distracted by some

books, and the girls were fascinated by the mirrors that reflected their delighted faces.

There were so many things; Josefina didn't know how she'd ever choose something for herself. Then Tía Dolores and the girls stopped in front of a trader who had toys among his goods. One toy in particular caught Josefina's eye. It was a little toy farm carved out of wood.

"Oh, look!" said Josefina as she knelt in front of it. There was a tiny cow, a horse pulling a cart, a goat, and a funny pink pig in front of a white stable. Two green trees shaded a painted house with a white fence behind it.

"You can almost hear the cow moo, can't you?" someone joked. It was Patrick. He and Papá and Abuelito had finished their business and had come to find Tía Dolores and the girls.

"I think the farm is very pretty," said Josefina. "I like it."

Clara looked over Josefina's shoulder. "But it's just a toy," she said. "You shouldn't waste your blanket on *that*!"

Papá stooped and spoke softly so that only Josefina could hear. "If that's what you want, then that's what you should get," he said. "Don't let anyone talk you out of your heart's desire." Then in a louder voice he said to Tía Dolores, "I have good news. Señor Patrick has found traders who want to buy all of our mules."

"Oh?" said Tía Dolores. Her eyes had a question in them.

"Sí," answered Papá. His voice was serious and sure. "I have decided to let Señor Patrick trade the mules for us. He knows the americano traders. He can speak English to them. And he has promised to get me a good price."

"My friends will be glad to get the mules," said Patrick quickly. "Mules do better than oxen on the wagon trails. Oxen get sunburned." Patrick pointed to his own red nose and joked, "Just like me!" Everyone laughed, and Patrick went on, "I can get you silver for the mules, Señor Montoya."

Silver! This was lucky indeed. Normally, Papá would have traded the mules for goods from the americanos. Then he would trade the goods for sheep. Josefina knew Papá must be pleased. It would be much easier to use silver to buy the sheep they needed.

"So, Señor, may I come by later today to get the mules?" Patrick asked Papá. "I can bring some of your silver today and the rest at the end of the week after I've sold all the mules."

"Very well," said Papá. "I know I can trust you to keep your word." He and Patrick shook hands to seal their agreement.

*Oh, I am so glad Papá has decided to trust Señor Patrick,* thought Josefina.

# A Charm from the Sky

## CHAPTER 7

L ater that afternoon, Patrick came to Abuelito's rancho to get Papá's mules. He was going to take them back to Santa Fe after dinner. Josefina had climbed the hilltop to meet him and lead him to the house.

Before they started down the hill, Patrick tilted his head back and said, "I've never seen a sky so blue."

"Mamá used to say the sky is that blue because it's the bottom of heaven," said Josefina.

Patrick smiled. "Yesterday, I climbed up to the bell of San Miguel Chapel," he said. "While I was up there, a little bit of the sky fell off, right into my hand. See?"

Josefina giggled when she looked. Patrick held a small chunk of turquoise in his hand. The turquoise *was* the same glorious blue as the sky.

Patrick tossed the chunk of turquoise up in the air, caught it with the same hand, and put it in his pocket. "Now I'll have a little bit of New Mexican sky with me even when I go back home," he said. Then he pretended to frown. "What's this?" he asked. He pulled a sheet of paper out of the same pocket and handed it to Josefina. "I believe this is for you, Señorita Josefina."

"Gracias!" said Josefina. The paper was sheet music. It had the notes and the words to a song printed on it. Josefina couldn't read the words because they were in English. She didn't know how to read the notes, either, which were lined up like orderly black birds on straight black branches. But she had seen sheet music before. Tía Dolores had some. "Perhaps when we go home, Tía Dolores will teach me to play this song on the piano," Josefina said to Patrick. "She knows how to read music. I think Papá does, too, unless he's forgotten." Josefina hesitated, and then said, "Papá used to play the violin."

"Did he?" asked Patrick.

"Sí," said Josefina. "He used to play when Mamá was alive. But when . . . when she died, he gave his violin away. I think he was just too sad to play it anymore. We were all too sad for music for a long, long time." Josefina looked up at Patrick. "It's been better since Tía Dolores came to stay with us. We've all been happier, especially Papá. And Tía Dolores loves music. She even brought her piano with her when she came up the Camino Real from Mexico City with Abuelito's caravan. You should hear Abuelito tell that story!"

"He promised to tell me some of his adventures," said Patrick as they headed down the hill to the house. "If I ask, do you think he'll tell me the piano story this evening?"

"With pleasure!" answered Josefina. She knew there
was nothing in the world Abuelito liked better than telling
a story!

It was with *great* pleasure that Abuelito told the piano
story and many other stories about the Camino Real during
dinner. Then Patrick told stories about the Santa Fe Trail.
He talked about herds of buffalo so endless, they made the
plains look black, and rivers so wide that you could not see
across them.

After dinner, Patrick took out his violin. He played
such lively tunes that he soon had everyone clapping their
hands and tapping their feet. He was right in the middle
of a song when, in one smooth movement, before anyone
realized what he was doing, he handed his violin to Papá,
saying, "Now it's your turn, Señor Montoya."

Suddenly, the room was completely quiet.

*What is Señor Patrick doing?* worried Josefina. *I told him
Papá didn't play anymore!*

But Papá did not frown. Slowly, as if he were both eager
and reluctant at the same time, Papá tucked Patrick's violin
under his chin. He held the slender neck of the violin in his
broad hand and delicately ran the bow over the strings. He
began to play, and chills ran up and down Josefina's spine.

*Papá began to play, and chills ran up and down Josefina's spine.*

Josefina sat still, listening intently, with her eyes fixed on Papá's face. Josefina knew that Papá's song was telling a story full of longing and hope.

Josefina wished the music would never end. Tía Dolores must have felt the same way. As the last note faded, she sighed a sigh that seemed to come straight from her heart. "Oh," she said to Papá. "That was lovely!"

Papá handed the violin back to Patrick and then smiled at Tía Dolores.

In that moment, Josefina knew what she wanted to trade for her blanket. She knew without a doubt what her heart's desire was.

She wanted Patrick's violin for Papá.

✾

"No," said Clara.

It was much later that evening. Patrick had left, taking Papá's mules with him. Josefina, Clara, and Francisca were in the sleeping sala they shared, having an argument.

"I won't," said Clara flatly. "It's just not sensible."

Josefina and Francisca shared an exasperated look. Francisca had agreed right away with Josefina's plan to trade their blankets for Patrick's violin.

"But Clara," pleaded Francisca, "we need your blanket, too. It will work only if we all do it. Patrick's violin is worth at *least* three blankets."

"I want to trade my blanket for something practical!" said Clara. "Something useful, like knitting needles."

"Clara," coaxed Francisca, "when we return to the rancho, I will give you all of my knitting needles. They're as good as new."

"Because you never use them!" said Clara.

"Didn't you see how happy Papá looked while he was playing Señor Patrick's violin?" Josefina asked Clara. "We have to get it for him."

"Señor Patrick will probably say no anyway," said Clara stubbornly.

But Josefina could be stubborn, too. "We've got to at least ask him," she said. She looked straight into Clara's eyes and said something she knew would convince her to cooperate. "The truth is, it isn't only Papá's happiness I'm thinking of. You must have seen how much Tía Dolores loved it when Papá played. She's been so kind to us. Don't you want to please her if we can? Think how happy she would be at home if Papá played the violin while she played her piano."

Clara groaned and flopped facedown on the bed. But Josefina knew that by now she was only pretending to be cross. "Oh, all right!" Clara said, her voice muffled. "I'll do it! May God forgive me for being so foolish!"

Josefina and Francisca smiled at each other in triumph.

They knew Clara couldn't refuse a chance to make Papá *and* Tía Dolores happy.

❋

The next afternoon, the sun shone brightly as the sisters and Tía Dolores walked to the plaza. Tía Dolores had stepped inside a shop when Patrick came up to the sisters to say hello. Clara had been clutching her blanket to her chest, but she handed it over without a murmur when Josefina and Francisca gave their blankets to Patrick.

"These are beautiful," said Patrick. "And they are worth a great deal. Why are you giving them to me?"

Josefina took a deep breath. "We were wondering if you would consider taking them in trade for your . . . for your violin," she said all in a rush.

Patrick looked surprised. "But I thought you wanted the little farm," he said to Josefina. "And you told me you wanted a mirror, Señorita Francisca. And you wanted knitting needles, Señorita Clara. You could get those things and more with these blankets."

"We *all* want the violin more than anything else," Josefina said firmly. "We want it for Papá."

"Ah!" said Patrick. He ran his hand over the blankets. At last he said, "Your papá is very lucky to have daughters who love him so much. I'd be honored to trade my violin for blankets made by such good-hearted girls as you."

"Oh, gracias, Señor Patrick!" said Josefina with a smile.

"It's I who must thank you for these soft blankets," Patrick said. Then he added with a chuckle, "That violin isn't very comfortable to sleep on!"

Josefina laughed and Patrick went on to say, "Meet me here tomorrow afternoon at this same time. I'll give you the violin then."

"We'll be here!" promised Josefina and Francisca.

As Patrick walked away with their blankets, Clara shook her head. "I hope we can trust him," she said.

"Of course we can!" said Josefina stoutly. "Papá trusted him with the mules, didn't he?"

✺

Though it was raining hard the next afternoon, the three sisters went to the plaza to meet Patrick. They stood exactly where he had told them to be. They pulled their rebozos over their heads and hunched their shoulders against the rain. Hour after hour after hour the girls waited, but Patrick did not come.

"What shall we do?" asked Francisca.

Clara shivered. "Let's go *home*," she said. "We've waited three hours. Señor Patrick is not coming."

"Maybe he forgot," said Josefina. "Maybe we misunderstood. Maybe we were supposed to come tomorrow."

"Maybe!" exclaimed Clara. "You can *maybe* all you want, but I'm going home right now!"

"Wait!" said Josefina. She saw a man she knew was a friend of Patrick's. She hurried to him, with Clara and Francisca close behind. "Excuse me, señor," Josefina said. "Do you know where Señor Patrick O'Toole is?"

"Patrick O'Toole?" said the man. "He left. Last night, the captain of the wagon train told the scouts to head out for the Camino Real. By now they're long gone." The man nodded a brisk good-bye and then rushed off in the rain.

*Gone!* The word echoed inside Josefina's head. She stood numbly, too confused and miserable to talk.

But Clara had a lot to say. "You know what this means, don't you? Señor Patrick has cheated us, so I'm sure he's cheated Papá, too! We've lost our blankets, but Papá has lost all his mules!"

"That's enough, Clara," said Francisca, her voice tired. She slid her arm around Josefina's shoulders. "Let's go."

Homeward the girls trudged. As they passed the toy trader, Josefina saw that the toy farm was gone. *Not that it matters,* she thought sadly. *Now I have nothing to trade for it anyway.* But that was only a tiny disappointment compared to what Patrick seemed to have done to Papá. *Oh, Señor Patrick,* thought Josefina. *How could you betray us like this?*

# Shining Like Hope

apá and Abuelito had gone to trade blankets for tools and did not come home until it was time for dinner. As soon as they walked in the door, Clara rushed to Papá. "Something terrible has happened," she told him. "Señor Patrick is gone!"

"Gone?" gasped Abuelito. "But he hasn't paid your papá the rest of the silver he owes him. He promised—"

"Señor Patrick's promises are lies," said Clara. "Yesterday Francisca, Josefina, and I gave him our blankets. He was supposed to meet us today to give us something in return for them. But he took our blankets and left! He stole them!" Clara looked at Papá and said, "He cheated us, so I'm certain he's cheated you, too."

"I knew it was a mistake to trust that americano!" said Abuelita. "We didn't really know him at all!" She turned to Papá. "If you go to town right now, perhaps you can find your mules and get them back," she said.

Papá's face looked hard as stone.

Tía Dolores spoke carefully. "It's possible that this is just a misunderstanding," she said. "If you reclaim your mules, you'll be saying that Señor Patrick is dishonest. If you're wrong, you'll shame him and yourself. You'll ruin his good name and your own as well."

"Sí," said Abuelito. "The other americanos won't want to trade with you, and you'll get nothing for your mules this year. You'd better be sure—"

"Sure?" interrupted Abuelita. "How much more sure could anyone be? Señor Patrick stole from your daughters. If he'd stoop to that, you can be sure he stole from you, too! Go now, get your mules back before the rest of the americanos leave, before it's too late!"

Papá spoke in a sad, tired voice. "It seems I have been wrong to trust Señor Patrick," he said. "I don't want to ruin my chances of trading with the other americanos, but I can't risk losing twenty good mules. I must do what I can to get them back. But it will be impossible to find the mules now, in the dark. I'll go tomorrow, at first light."

Abuelita pressed her lips into a thin, worried line and said no more. No one had any more to say. Soon after dinner, they all went to bed.

But Josefina was too miserable to sleep. Finally she gave up. She rose, dressed, slipped outside, and climbed the hilltop behind the house.

The rain had washed the air clean, and the full moon was bright, shining like hope in the sky. Suddenly, Josefina saw a shadow. "Señor Patrick?" she whispered, thinking wildly that he had come to find her.

But no. It was only a tortoise making its way to a *piñón* tree. Oddly, someone had left a piece of paper under the tree. Josefina bent down and gasped. *On top of the paper was Patrick's chunk of turquoise!*

With trembling hands, Josefina picked up the turquoise and the paper, knowing that Patrick must have left them for her. The paper was soggy, and the ink had run, so the drawing was blurry. When Josefina held it up to the moon-light, she could see that it was a drawing of a church. But which church? There were five in Santa Fe.

Josefina looked at the chunk of turquoise and remembered how Patrick had joked that it was a piece of the sky
that fell into his hand when he climbed to the top of . . .
*Oh!* Josefina pulled in her breath. San Miguel Chapel!
That was it! Patrick had left the chunk of turquoise on
top of the paper so that she would know that the drawing
was San Miguel Chapel. Josefina's heart skipped a beat.
That was where the violin was! Josefina squeezed her fist
shut around the turquoise. *Oh, Señor Patrick!* she thought.
*Forgive me for thinking that you lied.*

Josefina slipped and slid down the rain-slick hill. She
hurried across the courtyard and burst into the room she
shared with Francisca and Clara. "Wake up!" she hissed,
shaking her sisters' shoulders. When they opened their
eyes, Josefina waved the drawing at them and said, "Señor
Patrick didn't lie! He left this to tell me where the violin is.
He left the violin in San Miguel Chapel."

Clara and Francisca looked bewildered. "But why—"
Clara began.

"Señor Patrick put the violin in San Miguel Chapel
because he knew it would be safe there," explained
Josefina. "He had to leave Santa Fe in the middle of the
night. He couldn't bring the violin here and wake up the
whole household. He couldn't leave it up on the hilltop,
where it would be ruined by rain. He couldn't write a note

to tell us where it was because we can't read English and he can't write Spanish. So he left me the drawing and his chunk of turquoise. He trusted me to figure it out. I'll show this paper to Papá, and it will prove to him that Señor Patrick is honest. Papá won't have to break off the trade!"

"Don't bother Papá with that! It's just a piece of paper," said Clara. "It doesn't prove anything. Only the violin would prove that Señor Patrick didn't cheat us—and Papá, too."

"Then I'll have to *get* the violin, won't I?" said Josefina. "I'll go now."

Clara was horrified. "Josefina!" she sputtered. "You can't go into Santa Fe by yourself in the middle of the night! It's dangerous."

Francisca stood up and began to pull on her clothes. "I'll go with you," she said to Josefina.

"We'll have to hurry," said Josefina. "It'll be sunrise in a few hours. We've got to get the violin before Papá goes to town to take his mules back." She looked at Clara. "Promise you won't tell anyone that we've gone."

"I promise," said Clara. "But you must promise to be careful." She sighed. "If only I'd traded my blanket for those knitting needles!"

Josefina and Francisca crept from their room, tiptoed across the courtyard, and slipped out the front gate. They dashed to the road and then ran as fast as they could.

As they drew near the town, light shining from windows and doorways spilled across the road. The girls heard bursts of music, clapping, and the thunder of dancing feet coming from parties. "Let's stay away from the plaza," whispered Josefina. "Too many people—they might see us." Francisca nodded.

At that moment, the girls heard voices. A group of men swayed toward them, singing and laughing. Josefina and Francisca shrank into a doorway, pressing themselves flat against the door, holding their breath. Josefina's heart was pounding so loudly, she felt sure the men would hear it.

But the rowdy men lurched past the girls' hiding place and continued on their way.

Josefina lifted her lantern and cautiously looked around to see if anyone else was coming. When she didn't see anyone, she signaled to Francisca to follow her.

"What have we here?" said a rough voice. A tall man loomed toward them out of the darkness. "Two señoritas!" growled the man. He stepped forward.

Without stopping to think, Josefina tripped him, and he fell with a heavy thud. Josefina took hold of Francisca's hand and the two girls ran for all they were worth.

Just when Josefina thought she could not run another step, the moon-washed front of San Miguel Chapel rose up before them into the dark night sky. Up the steps they flew. Josefina grasped the handle of one of the huge doors with both hands and pulled it with all her strength. Slowly, the door creaked open, and the two breathless girls ran inside.

Trembling, the girls walked forward. It was cold inside the church, and at first it seemed darker than outside. But gradually Josefina's eyes adjusted to the dim light of the candles in front of the altar—and suddenly her heart soared with happiness. For there, safely placed against the wall, was Patrick's violin in its case.

*God bless you, Señor Patrick!* Josefina thought.

She grabbed Francisca's hand and pulled her over to the violin. "Look!" she breathed. Patrick had even tied a ribbon around the violin case. Josefina knelt down and grinned. "I think Señor Patrick knew that you would come with me," she said to Francisca. Because next to the violin was the mirror that Francisca had wanted.

Francisca smiled. "He left something for you, too," she said. She picked up a small box and handed it to Josefina.

Josefina looked inside. It was the little farm! All the pieces fit together neatly in the small box. Josefina touched the farmhouse. *Gracias, Señor Patrick,* she thought.

"We'd better go," said Francisca.

The girls stood. When Josefina picked up the violin case, something poked her hand. Josefina looked. Patrick had used the ribbon to tie the knitting needles for Clara to the case!

Josefina and Francisca smiled at each other. But there was no time to lose. When the girls walked outside the church, the sky was beginning to grow light. Josefina knew that meant Papá was probably awake and getting ready to come into town. She and Francisca had to get home fast. They had to stop him!

When they reached Abuelito's house, they saw that Papá's horse was saddled, and he was saying good-bye to Tía Dolores.

Josefina ran straight to Papá and held out the violin. "Look, Papá," she said, all out of breath. "This is Señor Patrick's violin. This is what we traded our blankets for. He didn't lie to us. He left the violin for us in the church. Please don't go into town! Please don't take back your mules. Señor Patrick is honest. The violin proves it!" She thrust the violin into Papá's hands. "If he kept his promise to us, then surely he'll keep his promise to you."

Papá was astounded. He looked at the violin and then at his two daughters.

Tía Dolores was the first to speak. "Do you mean to say that you two went into Santa Fe by yourselves in the middle of the night to get this violin?"

The girls nodded. "We're sorry," said Josefina.

"But we had to prove to Papá that Señor Patrick is honest," Francisca added.

"You stopped me from making a serious mistake, and I am grateful," Papá said in his deep voice. "Now I am sure that somehow Señor Patrick will get me the money he owes me for the mules." He paused, and then said, "Go inside. Your abuelita will have some sharp words for you when she finds out what you have done, and I . . ."

The girls hung their heads. They knew they deserved a scolding. But all Papá said was, "I must ask a servant to unsaddle my horse. It seems I won't be going to town this morning after all."

Francisca and Josefina glanced at each other. Wasn't Papá going to scold them? They didn't wait to find out, but turned to go inside.

"Wait!" said Papá. He held the violin out to Josefina. "Take your violin."

"The violin isn't for us," said Josefina. "It's for you, Papá."

"For me?" Papá asked. "Why?"

"Because," said Josefina, "it made you and Tía Dolores happy."

Papá looked at Tía Dolores, and Josefina saw something that *might* have been a smile pass between them.

❁

That evening, a friend of Patrick's brought the rest of the silver to Papá. Josefina and Francisca had only a peek at the man as he was leaving after dinner. They'd had to spend the day in their room as punishment for sneaking into town. The day had passed peacefully. Josefina was tired after her adventure. She went to bed early and quickly fell asleep.

Something woke her in the middle of the night. Josefina got out of bed, opened the door, and looked into the courtyard. A sound nearly too soft to be heard drifted on the cool night breeze. Josefina had to hold her breath to hear it. When she realized what it was, she smiled. Papá was very gently playing an old Spanish song on Patrick's— now his—violin.

The breeze blew the clouds away, and suddenly the courtyard was full of moonlight. Josefina saw that she was not the only one awake and listening to Papá. Standing in the doorway to her room, humming Papá's song, was Tía Dolores.

# Gifts and Blessings

##### ∘◌⟨ CHAPTER 9 ⟩◌∘

 fter their visit to Santa Fe, Josefina and her family returned to their rancho. Summer turned into fall, and then winter came. The world was dusted with white, glittering snow and filled with the excitement of the holiday season.

Early on the morning of January sixth, a whisper tickled Josefina's ear. "Josefina," it said. "Wake up."

Josefina pushed back her blanket and opened her sleepy eyes. She saw her little nephews, Juan and Antonio, crouched next to her, their faces bright with excitement.

"Look!" whispered Juan. He and Antonio held up their shoes to show Josefina. "The three kings were here! They put treats in our shoes!"

"Yours, too, Josefina!" said Antonio, with a mouth full of sweets.

"Oh!" breathed Josefina. She sat up quickly, and Antonio handed her one of her own shoes. In it, wrapped in a scrap of clean cloth, were pieces of candied fruits, slices of dried apples and apricots, and a small cone of sugar. In the toe of her shoe there was a tiny goat carved out of wood that looked just like Sombrita.

January sixth was the Feast of the Three Kings. The night before, the children had filled their shoes with hay and left them outside. The story was that the three kings would pass by on their way home from bringing gifts to the Christ Child in Bethlehem. The kings' camels would eat the hay, and the kings would leave sweets and gifts in the children's shoes to say thank you.

"The three kings were very generous to us," Josefina said as she nibbled a piece of candied melon.

Antonio sighed and Josefina saw that his shoe was already nearly empty. "My shoe's too small," he said.

"Antonio, you had lots of sweets," whispered Juan, who was five. "You ate them too fast!"

Antonio hung his head. Josefina felt sorry for him. After all, he was only three. This was the first year he'd put his shoe out. Josefina remembered how it felt to be the youngest and to have the smallest shoe and to be so excited that she ate up her sweets instead of saving them the way her older sisters did. All that had changed. Francisca and Clara considered themselves too grown-up for the tradition, so now Josefina was the oldest child in the family to put out her shoe. "You can have some of my sweets," she said to Antonio. "I need my shoe, anyway. I can't hop to the stream on one foot."

"Gracias," said Antonio. He popped one of Josefina's sweets in his mouth and began to hop around the room.

Josefina neatly rolled up her sheepskin and blankets and propped Niña on top. "You boys had better hop back to your room and get dressed," she said. "There's a lot to do to get ready for the *fiesta* tonight." There was always a big party to celebrate the Feast of the Three Kings, which was the last day of the Christmas season.

Clara was awake by now. She opened the door, and a blast of cold air as sharp as an icicle came through. "It snowed in the night," Clara said. "If it starts again, there might not be any fiesta."

Antonio stopped hopping, and Juan asked, "No fiesta?"

"Don't worry," said Josefina. Now that she was almost eleven, she didn't let Clara's unhappy predictions discourage her. "It's early yet. As soon as the sun comes up, the sky will be blue. I'm sure of it. Now go!" She shooed the boys back to the room they shared with their parents, Ana and Tomás. Then she pulled on her warmest sarape and headed to the stream.

Josefina fetched water for the household first thing every morning. Today fresh new snow squeaked under her feet. The noisy stream greeted her, rushing around rocks capped with snow. Josefina knew that the old saying *El agua es la vida* was true. Water was life to the rancho.

Nothing could grow without it. The stream flowed along as steadily as time and blessed the rancho as it passed.

Josefina filled her water jar with the stinging-cold water. She put a ring of braided yucca leaves on her head and then balanced the jar on top of it. She walked back up the path, thinking about all the delicious foods for the fiesta that this water would be used to make. There would be *bizcochito* cookies, spicy chile stew, and warm turnovers stuffed with fruit. Best of all, there would be sweet hot chocolate. Josefina's feet moved faster at the thought of it.

Papá met her halfway up the path. "Oh, it's my Josefina," Papá said as he fell into step alongside her. "I thought you were a sparrow flying up the hill toward me. You're in a hurry this morning."

"Sí, Papá," said Josefina, "because of the fiesta tonight."

"Ah!" said Papá. "Tía Dolores tells me that you're going to play the piano at the fiesta. She says you have a gift for music."

Josefina blushed. "Tía Dolores is very kind," she said.

"Sí," agreed Papá. "She is." They walked a few steps and then he said, "I can remember when you'd have been much too shy to play music at a fiesta."

"I am worried about it," Josefina admitted. "I don't think I could do it at all if it weren't for Tía Dolores. She taught me the piece of music I'm going to play, and we've practiced it a lot. It's a waltz. I'm hoping everyone will be so happy dancing that they won't notice my mistakes! I especially hope Tía Dolores will be dancing. No matter how flustered I get, if I can look up and see her dancing, I'll be fine. I'll pretend I'm playing only for her."

"I'll tell you what," said Papá. "I'll ask Tía Dolores to dance the waltz with me. Then you need not worry."

"Oh, will you, Papá?" asked Josefina.

"I promise," he answered.

When Josefina and Papá came to the house, they saw that everyone was up and beginning the day's work. Juan and Antonio were energetically sweeping the snow out of the center courtyard. Or at least Josefina guessed that's what they were *supposed* to be doing. Actually, they were using their straw brooms to swoop the snow up into the air. Then they stood with their heads tilted back so that they could catch snowflakes on their tongues.

"I suppose we should stop them," said Papá with a grin.

"Oh, please don't," said Tía Dolores, smiling as she came from the kitchen. She had a bundle of twigs, which she added to the fire already burning in the outdoor oven called the *horno.* "Ana has everything running smoothly in the kitchen. But we were tripping over those boys. They would not

*horno*

stop pestering us for tastes of food! They must have asked
for cookies twenty times! So Ana sent them out here."

Papá laughed and Josefina's heart lifted, as it always
did, to hear him. Josefina remembered how it was just after
Mamá died. Back then Papá seldom laughed or smiled. She
and her sisters had been crushed by sorrow, too.

Then Tía Dolores had come to stay with them. Josefina
looked at her aunt laughing along with Papá and thought
about the wonderful changes Tía Dolores had made. She'd
taught Josefina and her sisters to read and write. She'd
helped them weave blankets to sell and trade. She'd brought
her piano to the rancho and taught Josefina to play. Many
evenings Papá played his violin while Tía Dolores played
her piano. Josefina thought the best change of all was that
Tía Dolores had helped their family—especially Papá—to
be happy again.

"Come along, Josefina," Tía Dolores said now in her
brisk way. "Ana needs that water in the kitchen."

"Sí," said Josefina, smiling to herself. One thing Tía
Dolores had taught *everyone* on the rancho was her favorite
saying: *The saints cry over lost time.*

No time was being lost in the kitchen! Ana was making
turnovers. Carmen was stirring a big copper pot full of stew.
Francisca's sleeves were rolled up and she was kneading
bread dough.

"Bless you, Josefina," said Ana, taking the water jar. "Please help Francisca. I want the dough to rise while we're at morning prayers. The horno should be hot enough to bake the bread after prayers."

Clara was kneeling on the floor making corn flour. She put a handful of dried corn on the flat grinding stone and crushed it with the stone roller until the corn was ground into coarse flour.

"Clara," Josefina said, "it's sunny. There's not one snow cloud in the sky."

Clara shrugged. "Not yet," she said, crushing another handful of corn. Then Clara surprised Josefina by smiling. "It's not that I want to be discouraging," she explained. "I just think it's foolish to get your hopes up the way you always do, Josefina."

"I can't help it," said Josefina. "My hopes seem to go up whether I want them to or not."

"Like this bread dough," joked Francisca. She pressed her fists into the dough and pushed down. "No matter how I flatten it, it rises up again."

"Hope is a blessing," said Tía Dolores.

"Sí," agreed Ana. "I think

it's good to keep trying and never give up."

Just then, Juan and Antonio stuck their heads in the door. "Please," Juan asked for the twenty-first time, "can we have some cookies?"

"What was that you said about never giving up?" Josefina asked Ana. And suddenly the kitchen was full of laughter.

After morning prayers and breakfast, Josefina and Tía Dolores carried the fat loaves of bread dough outside.

"Oh, Tía Dolores, may I put the bread in the horno?" asked Josefina.

"Certainly," said Tía Dolores.

Josefina used her finger to press the shape of a cross on the top of each loaf as a reminder that all the earth's bounty was a gift from God. Then, as Tía Dolores watched, she carefully put the loaves into the horno and wedged shut the heavy wooden door.

"Well done!" said Tía Dolores.

"I can take them out at the right time, too," said Josefina, boasting a bit.

"Good for you!" said Tía Dolores. "You don't need my help with the bread at all anymore, do you? But maybe I *can* help you practice the music you're playing tonight."

"Oh, yes, please," said Josefina. "I'll practice playing the

*As Tía Dolores watched, Josefina carefully put the loaves into the horno.*

waltz, and perhaps you'd like to practice dancing it."

"Gracias," said Tía Dolores, laughing. "But that won't be necessary. I plan to be sitting right next to you at the piano while you play."

Josefina stopped and looked at her aunt. "Oh, but Tía Dolores," she said seriously. "Papá is hoping you'll dance the waltz with him. He told me so. You wouldn't want to disappoint him, would you?"

Tía Dolores slipped her arm around Josefina's shoulders. "No," she answered just as seriously. "I would never want to disappoint your papá."

Josefina was sure there had never been a more beautiful night for a fiesta. The huge, cold, black sky was sprinkled with stars, and the ground was silvery because of the moonlight shining on the snow. In the center courtyard of the house, a line of little fires lit the way to the *gran sala*, the biggest and grandest room, which was used only for special times like this.

Inside the gran sala, candlelight caught the bright colors of the ladies' best dresses and glinted off the men's buttons. Josefina and Clara were too young to dance, but they were allowed to sit on the floor and watch. Francisca swung by with her partner, and Ana waved gaily as she danced past with Tomás. The guests were friends from the

village or from nearby ranchos, and Josefina had known
them all her life. Somehow, though, their familiar faces
looked different tonight. Perhaps it was the gentle glow of
candlelight or just the magic of happiness that made the
ladies look so lovely and the men look so handsome.

After a while, Clara nudged Josefina. "Time to play
your waltz," she said.

Josefina stood, smoothed her skirt, and straightened her
hair ribbon.

"You look fine," Clara said. Then she stood too and said
kindly, "I'll go with you. Come on." The two sisters walked
through the crowded room to the piano. Josefina was
pleased to see that Francisca and Ana were waiting for her
there. They smiled encouragingly as she sat down.

Josefina had never played music in front of a large
group of people before. Her hands were trembling. Then,
out of the corner of her eye, she saw Papá bow and hold
out his hand to Tía Dolores. Josefina began to play, and
Papá and Tía Dolores began to dance. Josefina had always
liked the lilting rhythm of the waltz: *one-two-three, one-two-
three, one-two-three.* And tonight the music seemed to spiral
up, up, up in ever more graceful swoops and swirls as she
played. She never took her eyes off Papá and Tía Dolores.
It was as if all the other dancers had faded away. Around
and around and around Papá and Tía Dolores whirled. Tía

Dolores danced so lightly in Papá's arms, it seemed as if the music were wind and she and Papá were birds carried on it.

Around and around and around they danced. *Papá and Tía Dolores belong together,* thought Josefina. *They love each other.* With her whole heart, she was sure of it. Ana, Francisca, and Clara were watching Papá and Tía Dolores, too. Josefina knew that her sisters were thinking the same thought she was. And she knew they were wishing, just as she was, that the dance would never end.

# Sleet

## CHAPTER 10

**T**he bad weather Clara had predicted came howling in the next day. The sky was hard, dark, and gray, and sleet clattered and bounced on the roof of the gran sala. Tía Dolores and the sisters had gathered in the gran sala to dust and sweep so that the room could be closed up until the next fiesta. The day was dreary, but Josefina needed only to close her eyes to imagine the way the gran sala had glowed with candlelight the night before. She hummed the waltz to herself as she swept.

Papá came in with two servants. They were going to put Tía Dolores's piano back in the family sala.

"Wasn't it a lovely fiesta?" Josefina sighed.

"You know, I used to think a fiesta was hardly worthwhile," said Clara, sounding unusually cheery. "There's so much work to do to get ready and even more work afterward to clean up! But last night's fiesta was worth it."

"And just wait till you're old enough to dance," said Francisca, twirling around her broom. "Then you'll love fiestas as much as I do."

"Preparing for a fiesta used to overwhelm me," said

Ana. "But Tía Dolores has taught me to enjoy it. Now I think
it's a pleasure to cook food to share with our friends."

"You did a wonderful job," Tía Dolores said to Ana. "All
of you did." She looked around at the four sisters. Josefina
thought Tía Dolores's face looked pale, as if she had not
slept well the night before. "I am proud of you."

Papá spoke up. "Tía Dolores is right," he said. "Thanks
to your hard work, that was a fiesta we'll all remember
with great pleasure."

"Gracias, Papá," said the sisters happily. Such praise
from Papá and Tía Dolores was delightful indeed! They all
went contentedly back to work.

Except for Tía Dolores. She asked, "Do you remember
that when I first came here, I said I would stay as long as
you needed me?" The sisters stopped dusting and sweeping, and looked at her as she went on. "You've all learned
to do your sewing and weaving and household tasks very
well. And you all did so beautifully preparing for the
fiesta yesterday! I can see that you don't need me the way
that you used to. So . . . so I've written to my parents and
asked them to come here and take me back to Santa Fe
with them. I'm going home."

The room was completely silent. Josefina felt as if a
drop of freezing sleet were running right down her spine.
"But Tía Dolores, *this* is your home," she burst out. "We

thought you were happy here with us!"

"I am," said Tía Dolores. Then she squared her shoulders and spoke firmly, as if she'd made up her mind after a long struggle with herself. "But it's time for me to leave."

Josefina turned to Papá. Surely he would say something to Tía Dolores! But Papá only bowed his head for a moment. When he looked up, his face was composed and grave. He left the room without saying a word.

Tía Dolores watched him go. Then she picked up her broom and went back to work. But Josefina and her sisters stared after Papá, as if he alone had the answer to a question that was desperately important to them all.

❋

The more she thought about it, the angrier Josefina was with herself. Bragging about how she could make bread! Showing off playing the piano! *No wonder Tía Dolores doesn't feel needed!* she thought. The sleet had stopped, but it was still very windy and cold as Josefina walked to the goat pen to see Sombrita. "But I know how to make things right," Josefina said to the little goat. "I'll start tomorrow."

The odd thing was that her sisters seemed to have hit upon the same idea. The next morning, Francisca spilled tea at breakfast. Josefina was quite sure she did it on purpose. Francisca was wearing Clara's sash instead of her own, and the sash was badly stained by the tea. Francisca and Clara had sharp words about it, bickering just as they used to in the days before Tía Dolores had come and taught them to get along. Later that morning, Clara, who seldom made mistakes, snarled the wool, and four rows of weaving had to be untangled from the loom. Ana somehow forgot to put salt in the sauce, so dinner tasted terrible. Josefina made mistakes all day long. She dropped a basket in a puddle, forgot part of a prayer, and was all thumbs at her piano lesson.

That evening Tía Dolores and the sisters gathered in front of the fire in the family sala. Papá didn't join them. His violin lay neglected on top of the piano. *Papá might as well give the violin back to Señor Patrick,* thought Josefina with a sigh. *He'll have no pleasure in playing it if Tía Dolores leaves.*

No one had much to say. Then Clara dropped her ball of knitting yarn. She and Ana leaned forward at the same time to pick it up and knocked heads. Ana pulled back so quickly that she jarred Francisca's elbow, and Francisca pricked her finger with her sewing needle. Francisca yelped, startling Josefina so that she made an ink splotch on her paper.

Tía Dolores shook her head. "I see what you girls are up to," she said. "You're deliberately bungling things so that it'll seem as if you still need me. But it won't work. And you'd better stop before one of you sets your skirts on fire!"

She laughed, and the sisters had to laugh at themselves, too.

"But Tía Dolores," said Clara, "we *do* need you." Sometimes Josefina was glad that Clara was so straightforward.

"Sí," agreed Francisca. "Not just as a teacher but as part of our family."

"We were so unhappy and lost after Mamá died," said Ana softly. "And you made everything better."

"We need you because we love you," said Josefina.

"Bless you!" said Tía Dolores, no longer laughing. "I love you, too. That will never change. But you girls have come a long way toward healing from the sorrow of your mamá's death, God rest her soul. Your papá has come a long way, too. It's time for him to marry again, to give his heart to someone. If I am here, I'm afraid I may be in the way. That's why it's time for me to go. That's why I *want* to go."

"Oh, but Tía Dolores!" said Josefina. "Papá—" But Ana squeezed Josefina's arm to stop her. They all knew it would be wrong for Josefina to finish her sentence and say to Tía Dolores, "Papá loves *you*." Children did not say such things to adults.

"Besides," said Tía Dolores with her usual briskness, "if I am going to start a whole new life for myself in Santa Fe, the sooner I begin, the better."

The sisters could not look at one another or at Tía Dolores. There was nothing more they could say to her.

✻

There was, however, a great deal for Josefina, Francisca, and Clara to say to one another later when they were together in their sleeping sala.

"Maybe this cold, sleety weather will stop Tía Dolores's letter from getting to Santa Fe," said Josefina, listening to the wind whistling outside the door. "Then Abuelita and Abuelito won't come to take her away."

"Don't be silly," said Clara. "Sooner or later, Tía Dolores will leave. Didn't you hear her say that she *wants* to go?"

Things were always black and white for Clara, plain as a wintry landscape of bare trees and snow. But Josefina saw glimpses of color even in the starkest view.

"I don't think it's that simple," Josefina said now. "I don't think Tía Dolores truly wants to leave. She loves us, and . . ." Josefina swallowed and went on boldly, "I think she loves Papá. I think he loves her, too, but she doesn't know it."

"That's right," said Francisca. "How terrible to love someone and think he doesn't love you in return. No wonder Tía Dolores wants to leave. Her heart must ache every time she sees Papá."

Josefina spoke with great certainty. "I know that Tía Dolores would stay," she said, "if Papá—"

"—asked her to marry him," all three sisters finished together.

"Sí," said Josefina. "The truth is, I've been hoping he would ask her for a long time now."

"Well," said Clara calmly, "Papá and Tía Dolores would be a good, sensible match, and a practical one, too." All the girls knew it was not unusual for a man to marry his wife's sister after his wife died. The families already knew each other, and it kept their property together. "If they do decide to marry, they shouldn't waste any more time about it. Neither one of them is getting any younger. Besides, it's always best to have a wedding in the winter so that it won't get in the way of planting or harvesting."

"Oh, Clara!" exclaimed Francisca. "How can you be so matter-of-fact? You're forgetting all the wonderful steps in courtship. First, Papá has to write a letter asking Abuelito for Tía Dolores's hand in marriage. Then Abuelito and Abuelita ask Tía Dolores if the proposal is acceptable to her. Then—"

"Stop!" interrupted Clara. "You're forgetting that there's nothing *we* can do about *any* of this."

Josefina refused to give up. "There must be *something*," she said.

"Children are not involved in such matters," said Clara flatly. "It would be absolutely improper for us to speak of this to Tía Dolores or Papá."

Josefina knew Clara was right, as usual. Then she said, "But we could talk to Tía Magdalena. After all, she is Papá's

sister and oldest relative, and the most respected woman
in the village. I'm sure Tía Magdalena will come to see
Abuelito and Abuelita while they're here. We'll ask her to
speak to Papá. Oh, now I'm *glad* Abuelito and Abuelita are
coming! That will make it all happen faster."

Francisca and Clara started laughing.

"What's so funny?" asked Josefina.

"You are!" said her sisters.

"You find the sweet in the sour," said Clara. "The warm
in the cold."

"The soft in the hard," added Francisca. "And the light
in the dark."

Josefina smiled. She didn't mind her sisters' teasing.
She could tell that now they too were eager for Abuelito
and Abuelita to arrive.

They did not have to wait long. Abuelito and Abuelita
arrived from Santa Fe only a few days later. And just as
Josefina had expected, Tía Magdalena came up from the
village to see them the very first afternoon.

Before, during, and after dinner, Josefina waited for
a chance to speak to Tía Magdalena, but they were sur-
rounded by family all the time. It was not polite for a child
to draw an adult aside for private conversation. Josefina
knew she'd just have to sit and watch and wait and listen

and hope for a quiet moment. It was hard because she was bubbling over with secret excitement.

Juan and Antonio were excited, too. They loved to see their great-grandparents, Abuelito and Abuelita. The boys showed their happiness with their whole bodies, frisking and dancing about the family sala until Abuelita scooped up Antonio, held him on her lap, and sat Juan right beside her.

"These are the finest boys in New Mexico," Abuelita said to Ana. "I really think that they should be educated by the priests in Santa Fe. Juan is old enough, and Antonio will be soon."

"Sí," agreed Abuelito. "It's important for the boys to be educated so they can keep up. The world changes so fast!"

"And not all the changes are good," said Abuelita. "So many americano traders are coming to New Mexico now, with their different manners and customs and language! I fear our most precious beliefs will be lost if we don't do all we can to teach them to our children."

"Not all the americanos are so bad," said Abuelito. He turned to Papá. "Don't you agree?"

Papá nodded. "Señor Patrick O'Toole is an honest young man," he said. "I plan to continue trading mules and blankets to the americanos with his help. I look forward to seeing him soon when he passes by on his way home to Missouri."

"Then you will be interested to hear my news," said Abuelito. "I've been invited to join Señor O'Toole's wagon train and travel with it to Missouri. And I've decided to go!"

Everyone gasped. Abuelito went on with a pleased expression on his face. "I'll travel with the wagon train over the Santa Fe Trail to Franklin, Missouri. Then I'll ride a steamboat to St. Louis! I'll bring goods to trade and arrange for goods to be sent back here. What an adventure it will be! I guess I'm not such an old man after all!"

"May God watch over you," said Tía Magdalena, who'd been listening silently.

Abuelito smiled at Tía Dolores. "You know, my dear, I must thank you," he said. "I wasn't going to accept the invitation. I didn't want to leave your mother alone all the months I'd be away. But when we got your letter saying that you wanted to come home, I knew I could say yes. Because you're coming home to Santa Fe, I can go to Missouri with the americanos!"

*Oh, no,* thought Josefina. *This is terrible!*

Then it got worse. "I was glad to get your letter, too," said Abuelita to Tía Dolores. "Your father and I have waited a long time for you to come home to Santa Fe. It's such a comfort to know you'll be living with us as we grow old."

"I'm glad to be needed," said Tía Dolores softly.

*Needed!* Josefina felt a door slamming shut when she

heard the word. She and Francisca and Clara exchanged agonized looks. How could Papá ask Tía Dolores to marry him *now*? It would seem selfish, and it would hurt Abuelito and Abuelita. Tía Dolores would never say yes if Papá *did* ask her. Her first duty was to her parents. It would be unthinkable for her to let them down.

Josefina could not bear to hear any more. Quietly, she slipped out of the family sala, ran across the cold courtyard, and went to her sleeping sala. It was dusk, and the room was full of shadows. Josefina sat on the floor, hugging her knees to her chest.

She was all alone for a few minutes. Then someone came into the dark room and said, "Josefina?"

It was Tía Magdalena.

Josefina jumped to her feet and stood, head bowed, in the respectful way children were supposed to stand in the presence of an adult.

Tía Magdalena motioned Josefina to sit next to her on the *banco*. "All afternoon I've had the feeling that you wanted to ask me something," she said.

"Sí, Tía Magdalena," said Josefina. "I did. But ... I beg your pardon, but I don't need to anymore."

"I see," said Tía Magdalena. "I've invited your Tía Dolores to stay with me for a few days before she goes to Santa Fe with her parents. I've grown so fond of her, and

it'll be a long, long time before I see her again. Santa Fe is too far for me to travel. We'll *all* miss your Tía Dolores very much when she leaves, won't we?"

Now the words spilled out of Josefina. "Oh, Tía Magdalena!" she said. "It will be terrible if Tía Dolores leaves. It will be the way it was just after Mamá died, when we were all so sad. We were ..."

Josefina faltered. Gently, Tía Magdalena finished for her. "You were heartsick with sorrow," she said.

"Sí!" said Josefina. She spoke with conviction. "Tía Dolores mustn't leave! She belongs here! I was going to ask you to speak to Papá so that you could ask him to ... to set it all straight." Josefina shook her head. "But now Abuelito and Abuelita need Tía Dolores in Santa Fe. She *has* to leave. There's nothing anyone can do."

"Dear child," said Tía Magdalena, "I'm afraid you're right. Curanderas don't have medicine to heal such troubles."

Josefina sighed. "With all my heart," she said softly, "I want Tía Dolores to stay."

Tía Magdalena took Josefina's hand in hers. "Here," she said. She put something as smooth and cool as a raindrop into Josefina's palm.

It was a *milagro,* a little medal. Josefina knew that a milagro was a symbol of a special hope or prayer. When someone wanted to ask a saint for help, he'd pin a milagro to that saint's statue. If she were praying to find a lost sheep, she would choose a milagro in the shape of a sheep. To pray for a hurt foot to heal, the person would choose a milagro in the shape of a foot.

"I want you to keep this milagro with you," said Tía Magdalena. "It will remind you to pray for your family's happiness, for your sorrow to be healed. And perhaps it will help you not to lose hope in your heart's desire."

"Gracias, Tía Magdalena," said Josefina. The milagro Tía Magdalena had given her was in the shape of a heart.

# Josefina's Plan

## CHAPTER 11

E arly the next morning, Tía Dolores left Papá's rancho and went to Tía Magdalena's house in the village, which was about a mile away. It was a bleak day. The tree branches were coated with hard, new ice, and they clinked when the wind knocked them together.

All that day, Josefina thought that the rancho seemed to be under a terrible spell, frozen in gloom, even though everything ran smoothly enough. No one spilled tea or ruined weaving or burned tortillas. Dinner was well cooked and served on time. Josefina did not make a single mistake when she practiced playing the piano. And yet somehow, the music was all wrong. It was just noisy, clanging sound. There was no joy in it. Since the piano would soon be gone with Tía Dolores, there didn't seem to be much point in practicing anyway. There didn't seem to be much point in anything at all.

*This is what it will be like forever after Tía Dolores leaves,* thought Josefina sadly. She was wearing the heart milagro on a thread around her neck. Every time she moved, she felt the cool little heart touch her chest. It was like a gentle voice saying, *Perhaps there's still hope. Perhaps there's a way Tía Dolores can stay. Perhaps tomorrow you'll think of something . . .*

But the next day came and Josefina felt as dull as the weather. Fat gray clouds hung so low over the mountains that the snowy peaks poked through. Everyone seemed unhappy, except for Abuelita and Abuelito. Abuelito talked to Ana's husband, Tomás, about the new plow Tomás had bought from the americano traders and the new system of ditches Tomás and Papá had dug on the rancho to bring water to the fields.

"That Tomás is a clever fellow," Abuelito said to Abuelita. "He's not afraid of change. He did a fine job managing the rancho last summer while the rest of the family was in Santa Fe. I wish I had a manager who'd do as well for me while I'm away."

"Cleverness runs in the family," said Abuelita. "Ana manages this household as smoothly as anyone I've ever seen. And I've never known two brighter boys than little Juan and Antonio." She sighed. "How I shall miss them when we leave! I wish I could watch them grow and change!"

Josefina's brain seemed to wake up at that moment. An idea started to take shape. She thought about it all day and then presented her plan to Clara and Francisca that night as they were getting ready for bed. They sighed and shook their heads doubtfully when they heard Josefina's idea. But Josefina said, "We've got to *try*."

So the next morning, Francisca, Clara, and Josefina presented the plan to Ana. She spoke to Tomás, and then all four sisters went together to Papá.

Papá was in the family sala. He had a pen in his hand and Tía Dolores's ledger book lying open in front of him, but he was staring into the fire when the girls came into the room.

The four sisters stood with their hands folded and their heads bowed, waiting for Papá to acknowledge them.

He turned and said, "Sí?"

"With your permission," said Ana, "we'd like to speak to you, Papá."

"Sí," Papá said again.

Ana looked at Josefina, Clara, and Francisca. They nodded to urge her to begin.

"Papá," said Ana respectfully. "Would you honor us by considering an idea we have?" She paused. "Do you think it might be possible for Tomás and our sons and me to go to Santa Fe with Abuelito and Abuelita?"

Papá looked at the fire again as Ana went on. "Tomás could manage Abuelito's rancho while Abuelito is away on his trip to Missouri," she said. "I could keep Abuelita company and help her run her household. Juan could go to school and be educated by the priests. And Antonio, well, he will be happy to be with his dear great-grandmother who loves him so."

"Is this plan your idea?" Papá asked Ana.

"No," said Ana. "It was Josefina's idea."

Papá folded his arms across his chest and looked at Josefina. Then he asked Ana, "Is this what you and Tomás want?"

"Sí," answered Ana. "We'll be sad to leave here. But this would be a step forward for Tomás and our little family. I think it would be a good arrangement for Abuelito and Abuelita as well. It would be good for you, too, Papá, and my sisters because—"

"Because then Tía Dolores would stay here!" Josefina ended.

Papá's face softened. His voice was gentle when he spoke. "I think this idea would be wonderful for almost everyone," he said. "But I'm afraid that there is a problem with it. Tía Dolores has told us that she wants to leave our rancho and go to Santa Fe. If you go instead, Ana, she'll feel she's needed here to help run our household. It seems to me that all her life she's had to go where she was needed instead of where she wanted to go."

"But we don't believe that she really wants to go to Santa Fe," Josefina blurted out. "It's just that she thinks she should. You could convince her to stay, Papá!" Josefina didn't come right out and say, *If you asked her to marry you,* but that is what she meant.

"Dear child!" said Papá, smiling. "You have a great deal of faith in my ability to change Tía Dolores's mind!"

"Please, Papá," asked Ana. "May we ask you to think about our idea, and perhaps consider presenting it to Abuelito and Abuelita? They may have an opinion about it."

"I will consider it," said Papá. "You have my word."

"Gracias, Papá," said the sisters. Quickly, they left the room.

"I don't think that went very well," said Clara.

"He *said* he'd think about Josefina's plan," said Ana.

"But he has to do more than that," said Francisca. "He has to ask Abuelito and Abuelita for Tía Dolores's hand in marriage. She won't stay here if he doesn't."

"Well, he'd better do it soon," said Clara. "Tía Dolores will come back from Tía Magdalena's any day now. As soon as she does, she'll leave with Abuelita and Abuelito for Santa Fe."

"Oh, I hope Papá asks Tía Dolores to marry him," said Francisca.

"He will!" said Josefina. "I just know Papá will!"

Josefina's sisters couldn't help smiling. "Josefina," said Ana in her gentle way. "Don't get your heart set on it."

"It's too late," Josefina said cheerfully. She patted the heart milagro. "My heart's been set on it for a long, long time already."

❀

That very evening, when the family was gathered by the fire, the sisters watched Papá hand Abuelito a folded piece of paper. They heard Papá ask Abuelito, "Would you do me the honor of reading this?"

"Of course!" said Abuelito. He and Papá and Abuelita left the room.

"Did you see that?" said Josefina joyfully. "Papá just gave Abuelito a letter asking for Tía Dolores's hand in marriage!"

"No, he didn't," said Clara. "The letter just presents the idea of Ana and Tomás and the boys going to Santa Fe."

Of course, there was no way of knowing who was right. But Josefina was sure she was, especially the next morning when she and Clara saw Abuelito and Abuelita setting out to walk to the village.

"Oh!" exclaimed Josefina, hugging Clara in her excitement. "Abuelita and Abuelito are going to ask Tía Dolores if she accepts Papá's marriage proposal!"

"No," said Clara. "They're just going to ask Tía Dolores

how she feels about your plan. If she wants to go to Santa Fe, then Ana and Tomás won't go."

It was a blustery day and the whole sky was a pale, ghostly white, as if the clouds were full of snow waiting, waiting, waiting to fall. Josefina and her sisters were waiting, waiting, waiting, too, for Abuelita and Abuelito to come back from the village.

"What could they be doing?" Josefina fussed to her sisters. "Why is this taking so long? All Tía Dolores has to do is say yes or no!"

"*If* they're talking about marriage," said Clara, "which they're not."

Ana tried to soothe the tension. "Abuelito and Abuelita have many friends in the village," she said. "Their friends have probably come to Tía Magdalena's house to visit with them. And I suppose that Abuelito has told them that he's going to Missouri with the americanos, so they all have a lot to say. I'm sure everyone is surprised."

"Oh!" exploded Josefina. "In another minute I'll run to the village myself to see what is going on!"

"Heavens!" said Clara rather primly. "You can't do that. Remember, this is none of our business. Children are not involved in such things."

Francisca rolled her eyes at Josefina and grinned. They knew that Clara was really every bit as curious as they were, though she liked to hide it.

It was late afternoon before Abuelito and Abuelita returned from the village, just in time for evening prayers. After prayers, as they all walked out into the courtyard, Abuelito turned to Papá.

"Well, Dolores surprised us," Abuelito said. "We discussed the idea of Ana and Tomás coming to Santa Fe instead of her."

Josefina's heart sank. So Papá's letter had *not* been a proposal of marriage. *Oh, Papá!* thought Josefina, bitterly disappointed.

Disappointment turned to horror and disbelief when Abuelito went on to say, "Dolores thinks that Francisca and Clara and Josefina are perfectly capable of running this household without her help *or* Ana's! She says it's time for her to leave even if Ana leaves, too. She's coming to Santa Fe no matter what Ana and Tomás do. So we'll pack up her belongings tomorrow, and we'll leave the day after."

"Very well," said Papá in a low, even voice.

*No!* Josefina wanted to shout out loud. *No!* Tía Dolores leaving *and* Ana leaving? Oh, how could her plan have turned out so badly? With a rough yank, she broke the thread holding the heart milagro. She flung the milagro on the slushy ground and walked away.

# Heart and Hope

## CHAPTER 12

**W**hen Mamá died, Josefina had thought that the world should stop. It had seemed wrong to carry on with everyday chores, as if nothing had changed. But over time, she had learned that work was a great comfort in hard times. It was a blessing to do simple tasks like cooking and washing and sweeping, tasks that had to do with hands, not hearts.

Josefina felt that way the next morning. She was glad to go out into the biting cold to fetch water from the stream. She was glad the water jar was heavy and the hill was steep as she trudged back to the house. She was glad her heart pounded in her chest from the hard work, else she'd think it had withered from sadness. When Mamá died, Josefina had thought she could never feel that sad ever again. Now she knew she'd been wrong.

Papá met Josefina halfway up the hill. "Josefina," he asked, "I found this in the courtyard last night. Is it yours?"

Josefina saw something muddy dangling from Papá's hand. It was the heart milagro. Josefina frowned. "It was mine," she said. "But I don't want it anymore."

Papá wiped the mud off the milagro with his finger. "I suppose there's nothing harder to give someone than a heart she doesn't want," he said slowly. "Tell me why you don't want this one."

"Tía Magdalena gave it to me," Josefina explained. "She said it would help me not to lose hope in my heart's desire."

"I see," said Papá. He tilted his hand so that, just for a second, a thin ray of morning light found the milagro and made it shine. "I know what your heart's desire was, Josefina," he said. "When you and your sisters came to me with your plan, I knew what you were thinking. You wanted to make it possible for me to ask Tía Dolores to stay here as my wife. That would have made you happy. And it would have made me happy, too."

Josefina looked at Papá with a question in her eyes.

"The simple truth is that we can't always have what we hope for in life," Papá went on. "Tía Dolores told us that she wants to leave, and so we mustn't stop her. When we love someone, *especially* when we love someone, we must let her go if she wants to go. We must put her heart's desire before our own." Papá turned to Josefina. "Do you under-stand?" he asked gently. "We want Tía Dolores to be happy, don't we?"

"Oh, but Papá!" said Josefina desperately. "Tía Dolores doesn't want to leave. She thinks she should, for *your*

"Oh, but Papá!" said Josefina desperately. "Tía Dolores doesn't want to leave. She thinks she should, for **your** happiness."

happiness. She said that it's time for you to give your heart to someone, and she's in the way." Then Josefina gathered up all her hope and courage and told the truth straight out. "Don't you see, Papá?" she said. "Tía Dolores loves you. That's why she *can't* stay. Because she thinks that you don't love her in return."

Papá shook his head and looked away from Josefina.

*It's no use,* thought Josefina. She started to walk up the hill to the house.

"Josefina!" Papá called after her. "Do you want your milagro?"

Josefina turned. The heart milagro looked very, very small in Papá's hand. "No thank you, Papá," she said. "It's yours now."

✻

Josefina did not see Papá again until the midday meal.

"Josefina," said Papá. "Your grandparents are walking to the village this afternoon. They're going to bring Tía Dolores back here. I want you to go along to help."

"Sí, Papá," said Josefina, even though there was no walk in the world she dreaded more. She had no desire to help Tía Dolores begin to leave them!

Josefina, Abuelito, and Abuelita set out for the village under a winter sun so pale, it didn't warm the air at all. Josefina's nose hurt and her mouth had the bitter taste of cold in it. A mean wind made her eyes water, so she bent her head forward.

"Brrr!" shivered Abuelito. "That wind cuts through me! My hands are frozen stiff." He glanced at Josefina. "My child," he said. "Put this paper in your pouch and carry it for me." Abuelito handed Josefina a folded paper, and she put it in a leather pouch that hung from a string around her neck. "Gracias," said Abuelito. He rubbed his hands together to warm them. "Oh, how glad I'll be to get to your Tía Magdalena's house and stand in front of her fire!"

They were *all* glad to come into the warmth of Tía Magdalena's house. A cheerful fire crackled on the hearth, and steam rose in a cloud from a big kettle. Tía Dolores smiled at Josefina, and Tía Magdalena helped Abuelita sit next to the fire. "Come! Sit and be comfortable," Tía Magdalena said. "You must have a cup of tea."

"Gracias," said Abuelita. "You are very kind."

When they were settled, Abuelito said, "Josefina, please give me the paper." Josefina took the folded paper out of her pouch and handed it to Abuelito. He gave it to Tía Dolores, saying, "A letter for you, my dear."

As Tía Dolores unfolded the letter, something fell onto her lap. It was small and shiny and as bright as a spark in the firelight. "Why, what's this?" asked Tía Dolores, holding the little object in her fingertips and looking at it curiously.

Josefina gasped. *It was the heart milagro!* Suddenly, Josefina knew. The letter was a proposal from Papá! She was so happy, she wanted to jump up and shout for joy. "It's a heart!" she exclaimed. "It's Papá's! He's giving it to you. Oh, please read the letter, Tía Dolores! Then you'll see."

Tía Dolores began to read the letter, and her eyes grew wide. "Oh!" she exclaimed softly. Then, "Oh," she said again.

Everyone sat perfectly still, watching Tía Dolores. When she finished reading, Tía Dolores looked at Abuelito and Abuelita, and her face was lit with pure happiness. "Well," she said finally in a voice that trembled a little. "Josefina's papá has done me the honor of asking for my hand in marriage. Please tell him that my answer is yes."

"Bless you, my child!" exclaimed Abuelito. "We will."

Josefina jumped up and threw her arms around Tía Dolores's neck. She could feel Tía Dolores's happy tears on her own cheek.

❃

On the day that Papá and Tía Dolores were to be married, the sun shone down on bright snow and dazzled the world with light. And yet the air carried a wisp of softness.

Josefina took a deep breath as she walked up the hill from the stream. There was no mistaking the teasing hint of spring. She smiled to herself, thinking of the sprouts still sleeping under the snow, soon to be awakened by the spring sun.

This morning, both Papá and Tía Dolores met Josefina partway up the path to the house from the stream. They stood together, smiling, as they waited for Josefina to join them.

"Josefina," said Papá. "Tía Dolores and I want you to do something."

Tía Dolores pulled Josefina's hand toward her and put the heart milagro in it. "This is rightly yours," she said, "because you never forgot your heart's desire."

"Will you keep the heart milagro safe for us?" asked Papá, smiling at Josefina with love.

"I will," said Josefina. "I promise."

Josefina remembered her promise later. She held the heart milagro in her hand as she stood outside the church after the wedding ceremony. Everyone she loved most dearly was gathered around her. Brave Abuelito, who was about to set forth on a new adventure. Dignified Abuelita, who held her chin up as if she were wearing a crown. Tía Magdalena, whose kindness and wisdom never failed her. Sweet Ana, her devoted Tomás, and their lively boys.

Headstrong Francisca and sensible Clara. Josefina was sure that Mamá was there, too, in everyone's thoughts.

Villagers and neighbors, workers from the rancho, and friends from the pueblo cheered Papá and Tía Dolores, who smiled and waved. Musicians struck up a lively tune, and the church bell rang out joyously. A flock of birds, startled by the sound, rose up with a great exuberant fluttering of wings. Josefina smiled. She knew just how those birds felt. Her heart rose up with them into the endless blue sky.

# Glossary of Spanish Words

abuelita *(ah-bweh-LEE-tah)*—grandma

abuelito *(ah-bweh-LEE-toh)*—grandpa

acequia *(ah-SEH-kee-ah)*—irrigation ditch

adobe *(ah-DOH-beh)*—a building material made of earth mixed with straw and water

americano *(ah-meh-ree-KAH-no)*—a man from the United States

banco *(BAHN-ko)*—a bench built into the wall of a room

bienvenido *(bee-en-veh-NEE-doh)*—welcome

bizcochito *(bees-ko-CHEE-toh)*—a sugar cookie with anise

buenos días *(BWEH-nohs DEE-ahs)*—good morning

Camino Real *(kah-MEE-no rey-AHL)*—the trail that ran from Mexico City to New Mexico. Its name means "Royal Road."

curandera *(koo-rahn-DEH-rah)*—a woman who is a healer

El agua es la vida *(el AH-gwah es lah VEE-dah)*—a New Mexican saying that means "Water is life." It shows how important water is to people living in a desert climate.

fiesta *(fee-ES-tah)*—a party or celebration

gracias *(GRAH-see-ahs)*—thank you

gran sala *(grahn SAH-lah)*—the biggest room in the house, used for special events and formal occasions horno *(OR-no)*—an outdoor oven made of adobe

manzanilla *(mahn-sah-NEE-yah)*—the chamomile plant. It can be used to make a soothing tea.

milagro *(mee-LAH-gro)*—a small medal that symbolizes a request being prayed for or a prayer that has been answered

piñón *(pee-NYOHN)*—a pine that produces delicious nuts

plaza *(PLAH-sah)*—an open square in a village or town

pueblo *(PWEH-blo)*—a village of Pueblo Indians

rancho *(RAHN-cho)*—a farm or ranch

rebozo *(reh-BO-so)*—a long shawl worn by girls and women

sala *(SAH-lah)*—a room in a house

sarape *(sah-RAH-peh)*—a warm blanket that is wrapped around the shoulders or worn as a poncho

señor *(seh-NYOR)*—Mr. or sir

señora *(seh-NYO-rah)*—Mrs. or ma'am

señorita *(seh-nyo-REE-tah)*—Miss or young lady

sí *(SEE)*—yes

sombrita *(sohm-BREE-tah)*—little shadow

tía *(TEE-ah)*—aunt

# Inside
# Josefina's World

In New Mexico, when Josefina was growing up, children celebrated their saint's day instead of their birthday. After waking the child with singing, the family gathered to pray. Flowers were placed around the saint's statue. The family gave the birthday girl or boy small gifts and treats, and they might put on a puppet show or read aloud from a favorite book. In the story, Josefina celebrates the feast day of San José, or Saint Josef.

*Statue of Saint Josef decorated with flowers*

Children were expected to be quiet and respectful at all times around grown-ups, including their parents. When greeting an adult, children kept their head and eyes down and didn't speak until they were spoken to. But New Mexican children had fun, too. When they weren't working, boys enjoyed ball games and girls played with homemade dolls. A toy farm like the one Josefina sees at the market in Santa Fe would have been a much-prized toy! Although Santa Fe was small compared to most cities today, in Josefina's time it was the biggest city for hundreds of miles, and

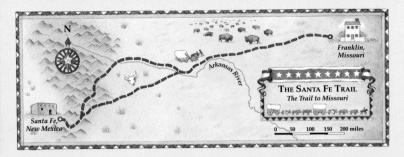

its plaza was the most important marketplace in all of New Mexico. Local merchants sold fine cloth, ribbons, spices, mirrors, jewelry, shoes, books, and much more. Pueblo Indians from nearby villages came with pottery, blankets, baskets, chiles, and other foods to trade. And by 1824, there was a new kind of trader: *americanos* bringing wagon trains full of goods from the United States.

The rugged route the americanos used became known as the Santa Fe Trail. It began in Missouri and crossed more than 800 miles of bone-dry plains and high, treacherous mountains. Like Patrick, some American traders learned

*The Santa Fe trail began in Franklin, Missouri. At left, American traders load their wagons with goods to trade in Santa Fe.*

*The Santa Fe trail ended in Santa Fe. At right, New Mexicans and Pueblo Indians trade their local wares for goods brought by the americanos.*

to speak Spanish so they could do business with New Mexicans. Some New Mexicans didn't trust the Americans, but others welcomed the new traders. American goods cost much less than items carried all the way from Mexico City. And Americans brought new items that quickly became popular, such as machine-made clothing and shoes. In return, New Mexicans traded mules, hand-woven wool blankets, and gold and silver Spanish coins. These items were prized by people in the United States.

The arrival of an American wagon train brought great excitement. People lined the streets of Santa Fe, shouting, "Los americanos!" In the plaza, traders enjoyed music, dances, and gambling in Santa Fe's lively inns. No proper girl or young woman went

to town without an adult to accompany her. Josefina and Francisca were very disobedient and daring to venture out to Santa Fe alone at night!

Although Americans were happy to do business with New Mexicans, many of them looked down on Mexican people and customs they did not understand. They began to feel that the Mexican lands to the south-west should belong to the United States.

*American trade goods included silk and calico cloth, shoes, glass bottles, cookware, tools, and toys.*

*American troops captured Santa Fe in August 1846.*

In December 1845, when Josefina would have been a young woman, the U.S. government tried to buy Mexico's northern lands, including New Mexico. But Mexico refused to sell. Soon after, the United States declared war. American soldiers took the Santa Fe Trail to New Mexico, and in 1846 they established American rule.

New Mexicans had very mixed feelings about the American takeover. Some believed that their chances for progress were greater if they were Americans. Others were angry and sad. When the American flag was first raised in Santa Fe, the women of the town wailed their grief so piercingly that even the cheering American soldiers were silenced. These women feared that their way of life and most precious New Mexican traditions would soon be lost.

When the Mexican War ended in 1848, the United States had taken the land that is now New Mexico, Arizona, California, Nevada, Utah, and Texas, and parts

SANTA FE

*In 1824, the purple area on the map belonged to Mexico. By 1848, it was part of the United States. The red line shows the U.S.-Mexico border today.*

*Josefina's friend Mariana would have lived in a **pueblo**, an Indian village of stacked adobe homes. In New Mexico today, you can visit ancient pueblos much like this one.*

of other states. The people living in this region—except Native Americans—were granted U.S. citizenship. So Josefina would have become an American when she was 34, but her friend Mariana would not.

New Mexicans, both Spanish and Indian, learned to take part in American life. But they also held on to their languages, beliefs, arts, foods, and faith. Today, the Southwest reflects the rich cultural traditions of all the people for whom it is home.

*A modern-day celebration of New Mexico's Spanish and Mexican heritage*